# BLOOD TREE

SILVER EDITION

SCARLETT DAWN

Editing by Rogena Mitchell-Jones Manuscript Service
http://www.rogenamitchell.com

Cover by J.M Rising Horse Creations
http://www.jennifermunswami.com

# ACKNOWLEDGMENTS

A huge thank you goes out to my beta readers, Jennifer and Sylvia.

You both rock so much!

# KENNA'S STORY

# CHAPTER 1

## *Age 13*

The screech of tires and crunch of metal outside had me running to the front window. I dropped my overnight bag on our couch and pressed my knees against the cushions, leaning over the sofa. My hands parted the curtains.

An unwelcome view was on our street.

I groaned and turned my head to the side, shouting over my shoulder, "Mom! Some idiot just rear-ended our car!" The trunk had been open for our bags—in preparation for our monthly visit to our cabin. The vulnerable part presently rested on top of my Mom's car, and the bumper was flush with the now-out-turned back wheels. "They fucked it up *bad*."

"Watch it, Kenna," Mom interjected, rushing into the living room. She dropped her own luggage and glanced at her watch. Her white brows furrowed, and she adjusted her glittery pink wig. At least it wasn't the green one. The fake hair on it looked like it came straight off a horse's ass. She yanked the front door open and stared outside…and then muttered under her breath, "*Fuck*."

I smirked and crossed my arms. "Watch it, Mom."

The door slammed shut.

When her eyes turned to me, I froze. I lifted my hands and stated, "I was just kidding. I'm sorry."

She gazed above my head, her eyes unfocused. "Kenna…"

"What?" I crossed my arms again. "I said I was sorry."

She waved her right hand absently, her attention still above me. At the clock above the mantle. "State the rules." Her eyes swung to the closed door, and she messed with the fake pink crap on her head again. "Now."

My mom was crazy. "Really? Right now?" I rolled my eyes, my voice dry.

"The rules, Kenna!"

I inhaled heavily. The words that came from my mouth had been ingrained in my head since I could remember. Insane words. "Never have sex before I'm twenty. Never open a black wooden door. Never kill anyone—even accidentally. And once I've had my period, never be around a man on the night of a full moon." My mom was cray-cray…but I loved her anyway. Pink hair and all.

My mom nodded once. Efficient and short. Her eyes were still on the closed door. "I need you to do something." I scratched my left arm, my regard caught on her chest. It was pumping hard, her breathing labored. "We won't be going to the cabin tonight."

"Um…duh." Our transportation was wrecked.

Her dazzling green eyes snapped to my identical green gaze. I scratched at my arm again. She had a predatory gleam in her peepers, her back straightening as she eyed me. As if she were on guard. "Listen to me. This won't make sense, but you need to do exactly as I say."

I snorted and forced a chuckle, my bones stiffening in awareness. "When do you ever make sense —"

"Shut it," Mom snapped.

Yes, something was definitely wrong. Mom never yelled at me. We didn't have that type of relationship.

She glanced at the door. To the clock. Then back to me. "Just do what I say this time. Just this once, dammit."

I swallowed and stuffed my hands into my pockets. My tone was respectful. "Okay."

A hard knock jarred the front door. But she didn't glance at it.

Instead, she placed a hard hand on the door, as if she were holding the person out.

Her voice was whisper soft. "Go out the back door, and then go out the back gate. Follow the white roses. The flowers will lead you to a love tree. A *white* love tree." Another peek at the clock. "At this time, you'll hear music if you get lost. Follow it. Once you've found the love tree, step between the trees." She pressed harder on the door as another bang announced the—obviously—unwelcome visitor. "Don't be scared with what you find on the other side. The people there are pure. Good people. You can trust them." She jerked her head to the back of the house. "I'll come to get you as soon as I can, but it may be tomorrow morning by the time I arrive." Another head jerk. "Go, Kenna. Now."

I stared, my lips pinching. I pulled out my cellphone. "I'm gonna call the cops." I pointed at the front door. "Whoever's out there is scaring you."

Her spine stiffened and she slammed a sharp finger in my direction. "If anyone is calling the cops, it'll be me. Now…go!" Green eyes narrowed. "Or I'm taking away all your electronics for three months."

My thumb paused on the screen. I peered up at her. My words were so slow. "Mom, past all the other weirdness you said, you want me to stay the night with strangers. Do you understand how *wrong* that sounds… is?"

"I know them," she huffed, placing both her hands on the door. "And I know these jerks outside. I'd rather you be with the other group. Not here."

My thumb hovered over the screen. "You sure you don't want me to call the cops?"

"I'm sure." With both hands on the door, she lifted her left leg back, pointing it at the back of the house. She waggled it in the air. "Get going. I have to deal with these idiots."

"Okay." I scratched my arm and pocketed my phone. "Call the police if you need them, though."

Her expression was pure exasperation. "*I* am the mother here."

I grabbed my overnight bag from the couch and walked through the living room. "I know. I know." As I shut the back door to our house, I heard the front door open.

Mom's words were muffled, but still loud. "Are you the morons who fucked up my car?"

I grinned and raced across the back yard. "Watch it, Mom."

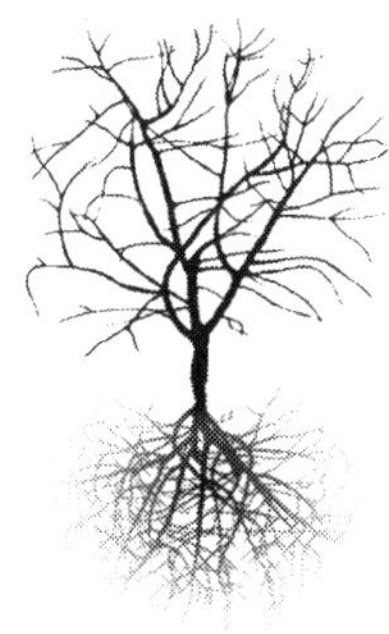

I was following a path of white roses. I couldn't believe it myself. The ridiculousness of the situation wasn't lost on me. Most people thought my mom was my older sister when they met her—because she appeared so young—but they didn't know just how weird she could be.

But she had never led me astray.

Or down the wrong path.

I snickered quietly. A 'path' of flowers tonight.

The sun hovered between the trees, just on the

horizon. It would disappear soon, and all I would have to light my way would be the moon. The full moon. Mom and I always went to the cabin on the night the moon was the fullest. *Away* from any men.

My bag rubbed against my side as I walked quickly. I kept my phone in my hand, just in case any creepers were out in the woods tonight. I usually loved this area, but tonight was different. This night my mom had been frightened by who she saw at the front door…and I had left her there.

Alone.

Just because she told me to didn't make it any easier.

Sometimes adults were stupid.

I kicked at one flower, the dirt fluttering up into the air.

I stared at the crushed white petals.

Lifted my phone.

Then placed it back down by my side.

I wouldn't call her. She had never made a mistake before. And that was saying a lot. My classmates' parents were always fucking up. The stories I heard at my private school gave me nightmares on occasion. Like real live nightmares. The kind that woke me in a cold sweat.

But my mom? No. She was always right in the end.

I kept walking.

White rose after white rose led me down a small hill. I pulled on a low-hanging tree branch to swing over a tiny stream. Up the flowers went on an incline. I dug my tennis shoes into the ground and used my hands to climb. Grass stuck to my fingers and dirt wedged under my fingernails.

I brushed my hands off on my jeans as I landed at the top.

I blinked. Glanced left and right.

All I saw were more trees in the setting sun. And the flowers.

But now I heard a gentle tune on the breeze.

It sounded like a flute. *Lots* of flutes.

Mom had tried to get me to play one of those in the school band.

And…she hadn't been pleased when I'd quit.

And…she wasn't pleased now that I had a boyfriend—thanks to all of my free time.

Actually, she wasn't pleased a lot of the time with my choices.

We agreed to disagree.

I tilted my head to the side. There was a particular tune that was haunting inside all of the others. I could single it out while the rest mashed together in painstaking revelry of the unknown.

I followed the unforgettable tune, my shoes trampling the white roses as I trekked through the thick brush, the crushed white petals left in my wake. My feet picked up in speed until I was in a full sprint. My bag bounced heavily against my side, and I knew I would have a bruise.

But that song…

I could almost touch it, the melody was so severe. It hovered around my body like a simmering flame from a campfire, heady and inviting. It pulled me. The music guided me, tempting me to find it.

"I'm coming," I whispered.

I was just as crazy as my mom—talking to music.

I shoved through two bushes. I stopped.

"Maybe she's not so crazy," I mumbled. My attention spanned the enormous white love tree before me. Its roots climbed from the soil, coiling and dangerous. I took care not to trip over them before grabbing onto the lower bank where the tree split into two. The branches full of beautiful leaves curved up and over the gaping hole, in a lover's embrace. I shoved my torso up…and tumbled over the trunks onto the other side.

I grunted and grabbed my bag.

Absently, I flicked leaves off my clothing.

But I only had eyes for the…castle.

"What in the hell?" I hissed, jumping to my feet. I barely noticed my legs were still moving toward the haunting song, my gaze glued to the freaking castle. Trees outlined the property I had stumbled onto, a massive evergreen lawn surrounding the out-of-place fairy-tale home. "I've never seen you before."

Understatement.

Massive spiraling pillars shot up into the air on the four corners of the castle, the gold at the tips glinting in the last rays of light. Windows splattered the sides of the structure, and open doors could be seen at the ground level, inviting any stray animal or person inside.

I rubbed at my eyes to make sure I was seeing this right.

My vision didn't change.

It was a castle.

Not more than a mile behind my home.

My house in Arlway, Minnesota.

Not England.

Or some other foreign place where they actually had castles.

"That's freaky-fine," I muttered. I lifted my cell phone and snapped as many pictures as I could while I raced across the lawn. Toward the back of the property. To the music. My pictures were going to be screwed up from the jostling.

But I needed to *touch* the music.

"Yep. I'm just as weird as my mom." My arms pumped as I ran. I peered off to the right and saw a man with white hair dancing as he played a flute. But I didn't stop. Though his music did as he caught sight of me, his mouth gaping. I kept moving, my body still in motion.

His wasn't the song I was looking for.

And he wasn't the first man I passed in my frantic dash across the massive yard. There were white-haired men playing their flutes, hidden amongst the trees or in gazebos. All were extremely talented. But none were who I was searching for.

I hopped over the last guy's legs as I entered the trees into the back of the forest.

He yelped in surprise from his seated position.

His shock didn't last long, though.

His unique melody charged the air as soon as I disappeared into the shadowed land.

I swiped at small branches.

Ducked under the larger ones.

The music…*the music*…I could see it. Literally.

White tracers, like smeared paint drops, hovered in the darkness before me, leading me to my destination. My fevered flesh cooled as I darted straight into the cadence of life. Because it *was* life. The currents on the breeze rushed into my veins, fortifying my tired limbs on their course.

I would find it.

I had to find it.

I needed to find it.

I stumbled on a rock but righted myself.

Only to be jerked to a stop by a strong arm curled around my stomach.

I kicked out. I was so close. I could feel it.

The heavy grunt from my captor didn't distract me. His arm loosened from my direct hit to his shin, and my feet were moving again. I reached out my right hand, running my fingers through the white music surrounding me. I twirled in a circle, giggling as the rightness of the night gripped my soul.

Until I halted.

My knees smacked the soft grass. My hands were not my own.

I pressed my fingers to the man's forehead lying on the ground. It was his music that I desired. The flute was pressed to his lips as he played *his* song.

My previous captor stopped directly beside us, his words quiet. "Oh. This is gonna be fun."

Eyes the color of black onyx shot open.

The man I was touching.

Our eyes met.

The white power floating in the air arced down, aiming straight at the two of us.

Captor-man jumped back, landing hard against a tree.

The music scissored straight through my chest. The man's own music attacked him too, shooting into his torso. The melody connected us, a line of pure perfection.

But…it was *so* much.

My mouth opened as a silent scream left my lips.

The white turned to black as my eyes closed.

My limp body fell on top of the man before me.

# CHAPTER 2

Someone was lightly tapping my right cheek. My eyes shot open, and I grabbed the unfamiliar hand. I blinked quickly in the darkness, my vision gradually adjusting. I stared up into captor-man's blue eyes. "Um…who the hell are you?"

His white brows rose, and he readily released his hand from mine. "I'm Randor."

I still stared. "Why am I on my back?" I tapped the ground. "Outside."

"You fainted. Outside." He tapped my cheek again and then altered his position to lean over the man who was lying next to me. The flute player. He was out cold. Randor was much less gentle with him, grabbing him by the shoulders and shaking him. "Wake up!"

The man didn't move.

I leaned up on my elbows but quickly lay back down. My head spun in a disgusting swirl. I swallowed down the bile, my voice choked with it. "He's not dead, is he?"

Randor stopped his shaking of possibly-dead-man. He glanced down at me as I placed my right hand on my forehead…and he laughed. It was all consuming, his knees even wobbling on the ground. "No. He's not dead." His eyebrows lifted again, eyeing me. His gaze lingered on my hair. "It's kind of hard to kill an immortal, kid."

"Uh." I must have hit my head hard when I fell. "Come again?"

"It's kind of hard to kill an immortal."

"What? Did you say…*immortal*?"

"Yeah." He shook not-dead-man. "That's what I said."

My attention lifted to the tree limbs hanging over us. "I bet you're friends with my mom."

He chuckled quietly. "I'm sure I know who she is." He paused. "What is her name, by the way?"

"Juliet."

"Last name?"

"Julius."

He nodded once. "She's definitely one of ours, but the first name doesn't ring a bell. I'll check the database…," he jostled helluva-sleeping-man, "…as soon as I wake him."

"Randor, why are you shaking me so?" Sleeping-beauty slapped at the hands on his shoulders, his tone irate. "Wait. Why am I on the ground? Outside."

Randor snickered. "You fainted. Outside."

Still too dizzy to move much, I lifted the flute lying between the man and me. I held it in front of his eyes—that were glaring at Randor—and asked respectfully, "Would you mind playing that song again?" My brows furrowed. "Though without the special effects that you guys put on. Something went haywire." I patted at my chest with my free hand, making sure there were no singe marks on my shirt. "I think we got electrocuted or something. There may be a loose wire around here."

The man froze, and then shot up to sit straight. His right hand went to his forehead, and he braced his body with his other arm. But his black onyx eyes stared down at me with an intensity that made me decidedly uncomfortable.

Too late, it really occurred to me that…I was lying on the ground. Someplace I didn't know. With people who were strangers. And they were men who looked college-age. In a dark forest.

I dropped the flute and rolled away.

My stomach turned with me, but I kept the puke at bay.

I grabbed my bag and managed to climb to my feet on shaky legs. "Actually, never mind. I think I'm going to…go." To the castle. I never thought I would imagine that. Much less, it be in my reality. This night was weird as hell. "My mom will be here soon to pick me up."

I couldn't see very well in the dark, only their white hair truly noticeable. And their teeth. Both had uncommonly white teeth. They must brush after every meal like my mom always told me to do. I wobbled on my feet but turned away. I started marching through the forest at a fast clip. Away from them. "Don't forget to watch for those wires!"

Flute-man grunted behind me. "Holy hell."

Randor chuckled. "That's correct."

"Samuel's going to despise this." Flutey snickered.

"And that's correct." A pause and I kept moving. "What are you waiting for?"

"She's frightened. We'll wait until she hits the clearing before catching up."

My legs worked faster. I leaned heavily on the trees—and puked behind one—but dang if my feet didn't keep moving the entire time. I hollered over my shoulder, "Stay back." I blinked. "Or my mom will kick your ass!" My mom, she was scary as hell when she was all-protective. "I'm serious!"

When I shoved past the last of the trees and stood on the lawn, I sighed in relief. The full moon was shining down bright on the grass, turning it a beautiful shade of deep green, almost silver in hue. The man I had hopped over first entering the forest nodded his head to me and never stopped playing…until a branch broke behind me.

My feet trudged forward again. I didn't spare a glance back. No need to. The dude playing the flute on the ground did enough for me, his gaze darting back and forth behind me. Two men. No guesses needed on who they were. I yanked my bag up higher on my shoulder, growling, "I said stay back."

"Yes, we heard you." The sleeper-man snickered, following directly behind me. "So we are. We are exactly one pace back from you."

I sighed, the castle so far away. "That wasn't what I meant."

"What's your name?" he asked.

When neither man advanced on me, I answered, "Kenna Julius."

"And your mother's name?"

"It's Juliet Julius," Randor answered for me. "It looks like Juliet became an Outsider the night after her Blood Tree almost fourteen years ago. She checks in every year with her superior, as is required."

I glanced back over my left shoulder. Randor was flipping through his phone, the glow shining up and on his face. He was a handsome guy, with strong features. And way too old for me to hang out with. I turned my attention forward, my steps stronger with each foot forward, my strength returning. "Is that the database you were talking about?" My mom had some explaining to do. A lot of explaining. "And who are you people? I've never met you, but mom trusted me to come here."

Sleepy-head answered, "Yes, it is the database for all Light Elves."

My feet halted. No one bumped into me. They were quick on their feet. "Light Elves, huh? Like *immortal* Light Elves?"

"Yes," he answered simply. "The database even includes those who are not twenty years of age. Those who have not reached their immortality from the Blood Tree."

I blinked, unmoving. "Huh."

Randor cleared his throat, his words quiet. "Actually, Ms. Kenna Julius is not in the database."

There were literal crickets chirping from the forest.

"She's not," music-man hummed. "That is interesting. Apparently, her mother doesn't follow all of the Outsider rules."

I dug my cell phone out of my pocket.

Dialed. Listened to its ring.

Only to get voicemail.

I put my feet back into motion as I left a swift message. "Mom, these people are cracked. Like, I really think they're on drugs. They're talking about all sorts of weird shit, and it's honestly freaking me out. Get here as soon as you can. I love you. Hope everything is all right." I hit 'end' and stuffed my phone back into my pocket. I decided ignoring the drugged-up men would be my best option.

Another hum. "Her mother hasn't done much."

Randor snorted. "Agreed."

A full minute passed in creepy silence before sleepy-hummer asked, "I know your name, Kenna. Do you wish to know mine?"

"Not really," I muttered, squinting at the windows of the castle. Lights were bright behind the glass. There were people inside talking or watching television.

All with white hair.

I glanced down at my long black hair.

I stood out like a sore thumb here.

"I'll tell you anyway," he murmured gently. "My name is Julius."

My brows furrowed. "Like my last name?"

"Correct."

I huffed. "What's your last name?"

"I do not have one."

I threw my hands in the air. "Of course, you don't."

He chuckled quietly. "You find that odd."

"Uh, duh." My nose crinkled. It wasn't nice to say, but this whole situation wasn't nice. "And you talk funny." I waved a hand in the air, regal and stiff, imitating him, "*Once a millennium ago, I came to be. For I am immortal. A damned soul to walk this dreaded Earth for all of time…*"

Randor chuckled but grunted just as quickly.

Julius ordered, "Acquire a new book on current slang."

"I'll put it on the list."

"You're supposed to tell me when I'm outdated."

"Sorry, sir."

Julius growled, but then stated softly, "If my language offends, I apologize, Kenna."

"Apology accepted." I eyed the first door. It was open like all the rest. I was almost there. "If I'm stuck here for a while, will you all be serving dinner? My mom and I usually eat at the cabin…but that went to hell." I paused. "Oh! Who do I need to talk to about getting a bedroom here tonight?"

"Randor will take care of it."

I skipped ahead. "Wonderful." Yeah, I would have to sniff all my food first. Who knows what one of the druggies might put in it. "Maybe someone else can take care—"

"No, Randor will attend to your needs," Julius stated, just as close as before.

I quickened my skip.

"Kenna, may I inquire as to your age?" he asked evenly.

"I'm thirteen-years-old." My lips twitched. "Seven years until I'm immortal, right?"

He sounded immensely pleased. "Ah, finally you understand."

I stopped just inside the doorway, light pouring over me. I breathed a sigh of relief. Other people were milling around the entrance that had a literal red carpet leading further indoors. A grand welcome for all. I snorted and tried to pretend I didn't notice how the chatter stopped as everyone inside stared.

At my hair.

I turned to say farewell to Julius.

But my entire body froze as I caught sight of him.

The brilliant overhead lights cast him into the spotlight.

Or maybe it was just *him*.

He was…perfection.

His white hair partially hung over his right eye, though his dark black gaze peered down at me with the same intensity as when he had first woken up. His eyes were large yet precious, with curling black lashes. His nose was straight except for the tiny crooked bump, like he had broken it once. His cheeks were flushed on his olive colored complexion. His lips were full, a little smile curving them—just for me. He was tall, way taller than I was. And his simple gray t-shirt and jeans looked expensive—even with the fresh grass stains on them. His toes peeked out of his flip-flops.

And he was far too old for me.

Luckily, he seemed to know this. He kept a good distance between us. No perv vibes.

My blink was ever so gradual. I swallowed. "Um, Randor? Food?" I sure as hell was flustered if I was asking a drug user to help me, instead of one of the others standing nearby. "I think I'll eat in my room until my mom comes."

Julius's red lips twitched. "I'm sure she won't arrive until the morning."

I blinked once more. "Because of the full moon?"

And he grinned. A full one. I had trouble tearing my eyes from it. He nodded. "Yes, because of the full moon." He waved a hand behind me. "And all of the men here."

My head swung back. Sure enough. There were only men standing around. Very handsome men. All too old for me. "Boy, my mom must really trust you guys."

"Nothing will happen to you while you are here." Julius placed his right hand over his heart, bowing his head. "I give you my word of honor." Those eyes flicked up from his bow, catching on the men behind me.

I took a quick step back…because gone was his gentle and polite nature. A dangerous man, with dangerous thoughts, lay behind those eyes.

In a quiet voice as he straightened, he spoke softly to the others. "She is *mine*. No one touches her."

My gaze widened, and I grabbed a handful of Randor's sleeve. I walked away from Julius, yanking Randor behind me. "Time for a tour. And food."

# CHAPTER 3

My mouth gaped open.

I didn't even care that it was embarrassing.

The castle was *amazing*.

"What is this room for?" I asked in full awe. There were brilliant chandeliers hanging from the ceiling. White love trees grew up from the floor in sporadic locations. Mirrors encased one wall, making the enormous room appear even larger. No furniture sat on the floor. It was all open space.

Randor chuckled. He lifted a finger and touched the bottom of my chin, closing my mouth. "It's for dancing, kid."

My eyes widened. "You mean it's a ballroom?"

"Exactly."

I sighed and twirled in a circle, my bag swinging out from my body. "It's beautiful."

He cocked his head, eyeing the room. Shrugged. "I guess it is."

I crossed my arms. "This whole place is incredible." I tapped my foot with each word said.

"You have ten entertainment rooms, three kitchens—six chefs, just as many dining halls, parlors all over the place, hidden alcoves from what I could see, probably secret passages too, bedrooms all over the second and third floors, and you have a freaking ballroom! This. Place. Is. Amazing."

Another shrug. "I've lived here a long time. It's just home to me."

My black brow lifted. "Oh. The whole immortal thing again, huh?" I snorted. "Just how old are you, Mr. Randor?"

The edges of his eyes crinkled. "My name is Randor Julius, not Mr. Randor. And I'm far older than you can imagine." He chuckled, his blue gaze running over my face. "Or seem to believe."

"Hit me. Just say it." I wasn't going to call him Mr. Julius. That was absurd.

"Let me just say I saw Christ come and go."

My mouth bobbed and my arms dropped to my sides. "Well, if you're going to go with the whole immortal story, you might as well include Christ, huh?"

He laughed outright. "Come on. I have one more room to show you before I show you to your room."

I held up a finger. "And eat. Those chefs looked like they knew what they were doing."

"I believe they do since they're as old as I am."

I huffed, following him out of the room. "So… your last name is Julius too?"

"All Light Elves have the last name of Julius."

"Of course, they do." I adjusted my bag on my shoulder as we maneuvered around all the white-haired men lingering in the hallways. "That's unfortunate for Julius then. Julius Julius. Sounds like a drink."

Randor patted my shoulder, shaking his head in humor. "No. Remember? He doesn't have a last name." He spread his arms wide. "Julius is the original Light Elf. All came from him."

My brows furrowed, caught up in the stupid story. "Um, I'm pretty sure it takes a guy and a girl to make another being. If he's the original, how did all of you come to be?"

Randor nodded. "Nice catch. When Julius and Samuel—the original Dark Elf—were born, they were each allowed the power to create ten new beings. Both Julius and Samuel made five men and five women." Randor flicked a finger at himself. "I was one of them." His smooth gate contradicted his arrogant tone. "I'm also Julius's head of security, his personal bodyguard."

I stared. "What would an immortal need a bodyguard for?"

His lips twitched. "Imagine being tortured for three hundred years. And never being able to die."

I shivered, my shoulders hunching in. "Okay, let's skip over the ways an immortal needs a bodyguard." Nightmares…here I come!

"True enough, kid." Randor stopped walking and tipped his head to the room we had entered. "This is the grand hall. It's where most of the Light Elves spend their time when we're not having fun on land."

Yep. There were a hundred men sitting in here, all conversing or on tablets or using their cell phones. Just simply enjoying themselves. "Wow." I spotted two people in the group…I leaned closer to Randor, and covertly pointed, whispering, "Hey! They have black hair."

Like me.

Randor winked. "Every so often an offspring of a Light Elf will show traits of a Dark Elf. It is a rarity, but proof positive that you're indeed Light is the fact you found our realm. Only a Light Elf will know the way."

I opened my mouth. Shut it.

It probably wasn't best to tell this guy my mom had given me directions.

Wait…was I really believing all this crap?

Randor spoke, pulling me from my musings. "I believe Julius wants to have a word with you before you eat and sleep."

I snapped out of it, lifting my gaze to him. "Huh?"

"Julius." He pointed a finger toward the front open door…and up. "He wants to speak."

My eyes traveled up. And up. "Holy shitballs."

Julius was sitting three stories up on an overhang, his head almost touching the domed ceiling.

"How did he get up there?" I squealed, grabbing Randor's hand. I pointed and jumped up and down, drawing everyone's attention toward me. The room quieted, but I didn't care. I waggled my finger at Julius. "What kind of drugs is he on? He's going to kill himself if—"

A scream caught in my throat.

Julius shoved his body off the ledge. And fell feet first.

He landed.

He didn't go 'splat' either.

My mouth snapped shut with an audible click.

His fall had been graceful. His landing had been beautiful—and silent.

His flip-flops clicked in the hushed room as he strolled easily toward the two of us.

Randor quickly released my hand, holding his behind his back.

I wasn't blinking. I couldn't even twitch my toes in my tennis shoes.

Julius stopped directly in front of me, in all his attractive glory, not one white hair out of place. He lifted his hand, and gently tugged on a lock of my black hair. With an adorable smile on his lips, he whispered, "Breathe, Kenna."

I swallowed and sucked in a large lungful of air. My words were so quiet. "Was that a trick?"

"No." He released my hair and bent to place his face in front of mine. "Everything Randor has told you is true."

My brows snapped together. "How do you know —"

He lifted a cellphone, waggling it in front of my face. "I told him to."

"Oh." I lifted a hesitant finger…and poked his left shoulder. He was flesh and blood. "Light Elves are real."

His words were patient. Kind. "Yes, we are."

My brows furrowed even further. “My mom lied.”

“I’m sure she had a good reason for not saying anything.” His dark eyes flicked to my hair. “She was probably waiting to see which you were. Light or Dark.”

She had still lied.

# CHAPTER 4

## *Age 16*

"What'll it be today, Kenna?" Mack asked. He adjusted his grease-stained apron around his rounded belly. The scent of cigarette smoke drifted on his breath and pieces of his brown hair were sticking out from under his hairnet. The heinous neon green light from outside my favorite small diner flicked through the window, casting a garish glow onto his wrinkled face. "The usual? Or do you only want desert today?"

I tucked a strand of my black hair behind my ear. "The usual today, Mack."

He tossed a burger onto the fryer. Sizzling steam lifted in front of his face. "Gotcha."

A menu entered my line of sight on the left. The man sitting next to me at the bar glanced at me, asking, "You sound like you know this place well. What's good here?"

I peered to the side. The guy was in his twenties,

with black hair and dark eyes. His features were simple yet elegant. He was handsome in an obscure way. You had to look closely to really see that his features were designed flawlessly. Otherwise, you would look right past him as ordinary. The light in his eyes sent a chill down my spine. My tone was dry. "Are you hitting on me? Or are you being serious?"

His lips pinched, and then he laughed. "I promise I'm not hitting on you." He lifted the menu again. "I'm new to this town. I have no clue what's good here."

His tone was honest enough. I pointed to the ham and cheese melt on the menu, but still left a good foot of distance between us. "That's good." Another point at the waffles. "Those are excellent. It depends on what you're looking for, breakfast or dinner."

"Thank you." He bowed his head in appreciation, and then looked at the lone cook. "Um, how do I order?"

"He's the owner, chef, and waiter. Just holler your order."

The man blinked. "That's new." He cleared his throat and stated loudly, "Hey, Mack!"

"Yep?" He flipped my burger.

"I'll have the waffles."

"Coming right up."

I twirled the salt şhaker on the counter, watching my burger and fries being prepared. "So, you're new here, huh? What brings you to Jonas, Florida?"

He removed his black leather jacket and placed it on the back of his chair, and then slouched on his seat, getting comfortable. "I travel a lot in my line of work. Jonas was just the next place to scout."

I peered straight at him. "What do you scout?"

"Baseball players. I look for athletes for the Minors."

"Ah." I flicked a finger to the north. "From the college here?"

"That would be the one. This town may be small, but they sure as hell breed some fine athletes." He smiled, and it was a little crooked. Maybe his only imperfection, if you could even call it that. "Twenty years straight they've had at least one person go to the Minors. In those twenty years, they've had three go right to the Pros."

I stifled a yawn. "That's fascinating."

He snickered. "Not into sports?"

"Not really." My resulting grin was genuine. "They bore the crap out of me."

"Maybe when you're older, you can appreciate the art of a curve ball."

I laughed this time. "Highly doubtful."

He shrugged but watched as Mack sat my plate down in front of me. "That looks good."

"It is." I took a large bite of my burger, talking around a mouthful. "He cooks the meat just right."

"Why didn't you suggest it then?"

I wiped away the grease at the corner of my mouth and then flashed the stain on the napkin. "Because your clothes are too expensive to have them dripped on."

He peered down at his attire. "It wasn't that expensive."

I snorted. "I know cheap, and that sure as hell isn't it."

"Well…thanks. I guess."

"No problem." I glanced at him again and chewed on a fry. "I'm Kenna."

"Jerry." He lifted his right hand, and he didn't notice that after we shook, he had a small ketchup stain on his right sleeve. I wiped off my hands afterward, evidence gone. He tipped his head to me. "It's a pleasure to meet you, Kenna."

"Nice to meet you, too." When Mack sat Jerry's waffles down in front of him, I snickered at his wide-eyed expression. "Hope you're hungry, Jerry."

His black eyes flicked to me. "You failed to mention it would feed four people."

I shrugged. "Mack's generous like that."

His crooked smile returned. "It would seem so." He poured maple syrup all over the gigantic stack of waffles. "So, have you lived here your entire life?"

"Only six months. My mom and I move a lot for her job, too."

"That has to suck for a teenager."

I shrugged. I didn't much like talking about my mom. Not anymore. "It pays the bills."

"Still sucks, I'm sure."

Yeah, it did. I finished off my hamburger and dropped a few bills on the counter. "Well, it's been fun." Jerry nodded his head to me, his mouth full. I slid off the barstool and waved to Mack. "See you tomorrow."

"Be safe out there, Kenna."

"You too, Mack."

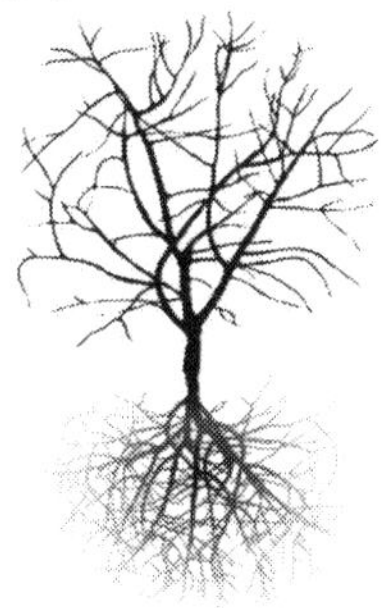

I slipped out the back door of our house. One of the many houses in the past three years. Mom had gotten a promotion, but her job had us bouncing everywhere now. These were less homes we lived in and more of a place we both slept in.

The door opened again as I walked across the yard. Mom shouted, "Where are you going?"

I didn't look back, my tone annoyed. "Where do you think?"

She was quiet, but as I stepped just beyond our property line, she ordered, "Be back by eleven. It's a school night."

I waved a hand over my shoulder. If I didn't acknowledge her in some way, she would come after me. It didn't mean I had to speak with her any more than was necessary.

She was a liar.

My entire existence had been flipped the night I fell into the Light Elves realm.

Sure, she had told the truth the next morning when she arrived. But it was too little, too late. My mom had been scared I was a Dark Elf and had hidden me from our people.

The thing was, in my opinion, the Light Elves weren't that much different from the Dark Elves. Both sucked energy from the humans to keep their immortality.

The Light did it with humans who were happy.

The Dark did it with humans who were unhappy.

Not much of a difference there, if you asked me.

But no one did.

Not even my own mother.

Instead, the Light Elves expected me to have the same viewpoint as they had. To agree the Dark Elves were an abomination, a blight on the humans. The Dark did create chaos to feed on just as the Light created joy to live on, but emotions were emotions. Where you have light, you have to have dark.

That was human nature. No one was perfect.

The Light didn't see it that way, though.

And from what I'd heard, the Dark didn't either.

I followed the white roses, careful not to trample the path. They grew back, but they took weeks to do so if I accidentally destroyed them with a careless footfall. The way to the love tree always changed, always moved. Anywhere there was an Elf, there was always a path to lead them 'home.'

I lifted myself through the love tree and hopped down on the other side.

And grinned. While I may have different views as the Light, I adored this place. The people here were honest, and I had friends in this realm, no matter how many different cities we moved to. The Light was always here for me.

This castle was my home.

"Kenna!" Susan shrieked, jumping off a tree branch—a high one. "I've been waiting an hour for you."

"I had homework," I grumbled. "It was geometry. I hate that shit."

My friend snickered. "Always with the cussing. Can't you cut down a little for me?"

"I'll try." I rolled my eyes.

"Sure…you won't." She grinned and grabbed my hand, pulling me toward the castle. "They're playing tonight."

I hissed, "What? I'm not dressed for it. I thought it was this weekend."

"Julius changed it. We'll be out with humans this weekend partying."

*Sucking their energy.* "Is he here tonight?"

White teeth showed as she smiled—a wicked grin. "He is."

My hand in hers started to sweat. "I haven't seen him in two months."

"I heard about that."

I dug my feet into the soft soil, halting our progress. "What do you mean?"

Wide brown eyes stared at me innocently. "Nothing."

"Susan."

"Yes?"

"Susan."

"That's my name."

"Susan!"

Her bottom lip popped out. "Your mom showed up here three months ago."

I froze in place. "Huh?"

"Okay, okay, this is what I heard from Jason. Simon told him he heard it from Kent—and you know he hears everything that Randor and Julius talk about." She inhaled so large, her breasts almost burst out of her top. She rushed to continue. "Anyway, your mom came here and spoke with Julius. Apparently, she doesn't want him hanging around you too much now."

My cheeks flushed deep crimson, already knowing the answer. "Why?"

Her tone was hesitant. "Because you started your period."

I threw my hands up in the air. "He and I are only friends."

She twirled a finger. "For now, you mean."

"That's the way it has to be until my Blood Tree," I grumbled. I rubbed at my forehead. "This is fucking embarrassing as hell. Can't she just stay out of my life?"

"Of course not. You're only sixteen." Susan flicked my black hair. "Until the Blood Tree declares you a Light Elf, your mom can't take the chance you'll have sex before you're twenty."

I ground my teeth together. "I've never walked through a black door before—and gone to the Dark Elves realm. Or killed anyone. Those should be the warning signs she really cares about."

She shrugged and grabbed my hand again. I was being hauled to the castle in no time. "She's just protective. As any good mother should be."

"She's a liar."

"Maybe. But she did it for you."

"Whatever. She still keeps lying. She didn't even tell me she came here to talk to Julius."

"Have you two actually been chatting?"

I stayed quiet.

"That's what I thought."

I ignored her snide comment. "You know what? I find it odd that there are all types of signs for the Dark Elves, but there is only the one for a Light Elf."

She shrugged a dainty shoulder. "That's the way it's always been."

Archaic is the way it has always been.

But I didn't voice my opinion this time.

I had more pressing worries tonight.

Julius knew I had started my period. I had no clue what I was going to say to him. I mean, he was avoiding me because, essentially, blood came out my vagina now.

Mom couldn't have embarrassed me more if she tried.

I squeezed Susan's hand tighter. She was the only one I would ever let know I was nervous. "Has…he said anything about me?"

"Who? Your mate?"

I swallowed heavily. "Yeah. That one."

Julius was my mate. He was my future, my forever.

The night I had met him during his bond call—to his one true mate—had ensured he was mine. And I was his. The magic of the music had claimed us.

"He hasn't said anything outright, but he has been in a foul mood." She wiggled her shoulders at me as we stepped inside the entrance to the grand hall. "I think he misses you."

The smile that lifted my lips was righteous. "He should since he's been avoiding me."

"Hey, kid." Randor stepped up beside us, lifting his left arm to me. "I've been sent to escort you to the ballroom."

"Randor, it's always a pleasure." My lips twitched as I linked my arm with his. "Susan, are you ready?"

She stood mute. Her cheeks flushed on her lovely face.

Like always, she became my silent friend when Randor was nearby. It was evil of me, but I thoroughly enjoyed making her squirm. "Cat got your tongue?"

Her eyes narrowed.

I laughed and nodded to Randor. "Take me to the ball." I gestured to my torn jeans, tank top, and tennis shoes. "I'm obviously overdressed for it."

"Obviously." Randor smirked. Then he held out his other arm to Susan. "Are you coming?"

Like a bobbing butterfly, her head sprang up and down in affirmation. It was damn hard not to smack her from her stupidity—and she was two hundred years older than me. She linked her arm through his, not saying a word.

"Well, since Susan won't shut up, maybe we should head to the music to drown out her blathering?" I yanked on Randor's arm. "Let's go."

# CHAPTER 5

The simplicity and elegance of the music caught my attention as we walked into the ballroom. It delighted and tantalized every cell in my bones. Magic. Power. The chords were laced with pleasure and delight, making my toes curl inside my shoes, an itch to dance crackled the air. The hair on my arms stood up, and goose bumps pebbled my flesh.

Light Elves wore ball gowns of decadent colors while the men wore white and silver tuxes, their colors swirling in a rainbow of enchantment as they twirled around the dance floor.

"Julius has outdone himself tonight. It's beautiful."

"Tell him yourself," Randor murmured, shoving me forward with a light touch.

I stumbled forward, but my hands grabbed onto muscled arms. Warm arms that encased my waist. A soft embrace, sweet and chaste. I peered up into warm onyx eyes. My entire face flushed in excitement, but I kept my voice calm and even. "I'm surprised to see you here tonight."

One white brow lifted, and he didn't remove his steadying arms from around my waist. I held still in shock, Julius never touching me more than was necessary. He stepped forward, placing our bodies an inch apart. His tone was low and quiet. "I needed to see you."

I scratched at my right arm, my forearm rubbing his chest in the process. "Is that an apology?"

"No." Simple. Sweet. To the point. "You know why we have to be careful now."

I sighed and barely kept myself from leaning into him. "We're only friends."

"True. But that could quickly change. I don't want to take any chances." He brushed his index finger over my cheek, and my resulting shiver had my fingers curling into fists. "You're almost there." A quick shake of his head. "But not quite."

I glared. "Are we going to dance? Or are we going to talk all night?"

"How about we do both?"

My eyes widened.

He cleared his throat, his eyes crinkling at the corners. "Until your curfew, I mean."

I growled under my breath. "Mom called you?"

"She did."

"She can suck it."

"You're always so eloquent, Kenna. And I think I'll wait until you're older to respond to your endearing comment about your mother." He chuckled as my mouth gaped. But my surprise at his crudeness quickly turned to joy when he twirled us into the dancing fray. I tilted my head back and laughed, knowing he would guide me without harm through the crush. We had danced a hundred times before, and this time was no different. It was thrilling even as we took care to keep any true *closeness* from occurring. Friends, first and foremost. Always.

When the music drifted into a slow tune, I whispered, "Is Susan staring at Randor?"

His lips curled in a chuckle. "What do you think?"

"Who's he dancing with this time?"

"Dana."

I kept my expression serene as I glanced over my shoulder, swaying gently in his arms to the loving beat. "Oh, she looks pissed."

"One day, they'll be together. He just needs to quit his wicked ways with the other women, and she needs to grow a backbone."

I peered back up into his eyes, my brows furrowing. "You know, we've never spoken about that topic before." I scratched at my arm. "Are you…"

He placed his mouth close to my right ear as he maneuvered us into a complicated dance step, twisting and turning us through the masses. "No, I'm not. I know who I belong to."

My heart beat heavily inside my chest. "Just checking."

His nose touched my temple as he lifted, and then he was stepping away from me, taking his heat with him. He tilted his head to one of the open doors. "I think I need some air. Would you care to join me?"

I nodded. "It is pretty hot in here."

He yanked on his collar, muttering under his breath, "*Fuck yes it is.*" I blinked, and he gestured for me to walk ahead of him. Soft silks and sequins from dresses brushed along my arms as I strolled to the exit. When we stepped out into the night, the breeze was welcome against my heated skin. He tipped his head to the small lake on the east side of the property. "Does that work for you?"

"That's perfect."

We walked in companionable silence over the soft grass, the moon shining its crescent glow upon us. When we reached 'our spot' at the third dock, we walked over the swaying wood to the small picnic table at the end of the platform. The dark water gently splashed below us, creating a white noise to the music still floating on the air currents.

He removed his suit jacket and placed it on the table, then loosened his silver tie. "So how have you been, my Kenna?"

"It's been quiet. Not too much has been going on."

"Your school studies?"

I hesitated. "I'm passing."

He leaned forward on the table, staring directly into my eyes. "How's your math class?"

I sighed heavily, dropping my forehead onto my palms. "Have you been checking my grades again?"

"You already know the answer to that."

"Dammit." I thrust a pointed finger in his direction. "And I've told you before, that's creepy."

"That teacher is an asshole."

I blinked. "How do you know that?"

He shrugged.

"Julius…"

"I may have visited him one night in his dreams. There was hardly any goodness in him for me to steal." He shrugged a muscled shoulder. "I left him with what he had. He needed it."

My jaw dropped. "Seriously?"

"Yes, his energy was so dark—"

"No. That's not what I meant." I waved my hands in the air. "Did you seriously sneak in on one of my teachers because I was failing his class?"

He held up a stopping hand. "I meant him no foul intent. I merely wanted to know what type of man could possibly be failing you."

I cleared my throat.

His onyx eyes were ruthless.

"Julius."

"Fine, I may have guided him."

"In what way?"

"To give you special attention so you would pass."

My tone was incredulous. "You're guiding him to give me a passing grade?"

"No, just extra work so you may pass on your own. And learn what you don't understand, thanks to his horrible teaching methods."

"My extra credit projects this month?"

"Yes, those."

I tapped my fingers on the table. "I guess that's fine."

He shrugged a shoulder, not commenting. He would do it anyway without my permission. He knew it, and I knew it. He was merely pacifying me right now.

"Will I ever win an argument with you?"

He hummed, an adorable smile lifting his lips. "Maybe in a thousand years."

"Oh." My brows lifted, and I snapped my fingers. "Just like that, huh?"

"Just like that." His gaze ran over my features slowly, and then he cleared his throat and peered out to the water. He stared and grinned, then flicked a hand in the direction he was watching. "Look, my Kenna."

I yanked my gaze away from his captivating profile and turned my attention to the lake. "My God." Gentle waves rippled from the indulgent breeze, and the moon reflected on it, the water appearing ablaze with white fire. "That is beautiful."

His dark eyes met mine, holding for long moments. "Yes. Beauty is finally here."

# CHAPTER 6

## *Age 19*

I was done waiting. In only two days' time, on my twentieth birthday, the Blood Tree would call to me. Julius and I had been safe, always staying just a step apart for too many damn years. My—*our*—waiting was over. Tonight, I was going to take charge for once.

Not he or my mother was going to stop me.

It was immoral of me, but a little anarchy never hurt anyone. If anything, it kept the spirit alive, living on the edge. Existing in an ordinary life was just boring.

And Julius and I would never be boring if I had my way. I wanted our lifc together to be full of surprises, happiness, or even the occasional heartache. When you lived forever, being 'bored' was a dangerous subject to everyone around you.

So, tonight…yes, tonight, I was going to be spontaneous. *Living.*

Slipping past my mom had been easy. We had gone to a lake house just outside of Jonas, like normal, on a full moon since we had stopped moving years ago—the college town our permanent address. When she had fallen asleep, I snuck out and followed the white roses outside the front door. The white love tree had been there at the end of the path, always waiting.

Sneaking onto the castle's property had been more interesting.

Even though I darted in and out of shadows, the men playing their bond call had stopped whenever I got within twenty feet of them—even though they couldn't see me. I'd never been around a man during a full moon, but I was beginning to understand why my mom had ordered me to stay away from them. I must smell like a damn dog in heat because at least ten guys had lifted their noses into the air and sniffed.

I ran like hell.

I was pretty sure one was still following me somewhere, but I focused on the castle itself now.

I knew many of the secret passageways—there were a ton—but staying clear of any man but the one I actually wanted was going to prove difficult if the previous bond callers were any indication. Any man outside the passageway doors would smell me…or whatever it was.

I would just have to be extremely quick. I knew Julius was in his bedroom working—a quick phone call had taken care of that information—so I would have to make it to the third floor in a hurry. I pulled my backpack tighter against my shoulders and raced inside the least used door at the back of the castle.

The lights were bright on me, showcasing I had arrived, but I instantly slipped into the first hidden passage just inside the entrance. My legs pumped as I sprinted up the spiraling staircase. At the small landing, I swiftly dug my fingers into the dirt, finding the lever to release the boxed door in front of me. It swung open and dust fanned my face and filled my lungs.

I swallowed down a cough and crawled through silently to a hallway.

Again, the light damn near blinded me, but I closed the hidden door and raced down the hall. This was the most dangerous area. Bedrooms spanned both sides of the hall—the single men's section of the castle. Laughter boomed and floors creaked as I ran by the closed doors…but the noises stopped all too quickly.

Almost there. Almost there.

I turned the corner just as I heard the first door open. I yanked on the edge of the third medieval portrait hanging on the wall on the right side. It flew at me, and I barely caught it before it crashed into my nose. Blood was not sexy.

I jumped into the hidden chamber and wrenched the picture back into place. I didn't wait to find out if the feet I heard pounding down the hallway would pass by or stop at the secret entry. Like a sneaky cat, I jumped up, grabbed onto the ladder and began climbing to the third floor. There was no light in here so I had to be careful not to slip.

I grunted when I reached the top, balancing on

my tiptoes to reach the lever to open the bookcase stopping me from entering the room beyond. I grappled with the hinge until it clicked, loud and ominous.

The bookcase swung open.

I toppled inside, landing straight on my face.

Not exactly graceful, but I quickly lifted to my knees, scanning the alcove.

There was a man in here. He was sleeping on the couch, his feet propped up on one end of it. I was pretty sure I saw drool on the corner of his mouth. And he was definitely snoring. Like, shake the walls snoring.

My lips twitched.

It was Kent, Julius's second in command of security.

Not so secure tonight.

I jumped to my feet and noiselessly shut the bookcase.

But my eyes narrowed when his nose twitched. If he woke up, I would be in trouble. He was a big ass dude, with muscles to spare. There would be no way I could get away from him.

I slipped from the room and raced down the banister walkway. It overlooked one of the common areas—where *many* men were sitting far below on the first floor. All peered up at me at the same time, their bodies tensing.

They froze for a heartbeat, their expressions quickly turning to horror as they saw me.

It was the same look Randor wore far down the hallway.

Where he guarded Julius's bedroom door.

His hands flew up. "Stop! Don't come near me!"

If it had been any other day, that would be funny as hell.

He was actually scared. All of the men were.

Because of who I was. To Julius.

His order didn't stop me.

I kept running straight at him.

He pinched his nose and held his breath, his cheeks puffed out. His feet pattered on the ground like he didn't know what to do. Right before I reached him, his face turning bright red from holding his breath so long, he grabbed the door handle and pushed the door open. His hand landed on my backpack, and he shoved me into the bedroom, slamming the door closed behind me.

"Lock the door," he shouted, his voice breathless.

I stopped dead in my tracks, my chest heaving.

I flipped the lock on the door.

Julius sat father into the room, his back to me as he worked at his desk. But he had frozen in place, the muscles tensing underneath his white shirt. With his head bowed over his work, the snap of a pencil breaking echoed inside the room.

His tone was nothing I had ever heard before. His voice growled through the air with sure death as the undertone. "Get the fuck out of my room."

My breathing labored, I placed my hands on my

knees. "That's a hell of a welcome after what I've been through to get here. But at least I know you're loyal."

His muscles clenched even further. "Kenna?"

"It's me." I cleared my throat and shoved to stand straight. "I've come to seduce you."

It was quiet for a minuscule second before I shrieked. Within a blink, he was standing in front of me, shoving me brutally against his door. My backpack banged against it, stopping our progress. His hands… his heated hands ran up my arms. Over my neck. His thumbs tilted my head back, making me peer straight up at him.

His eyes were on fire with hunger.

A wicked grin tilted his lips. "My Kenna, you have no idea what's in store for you."

I licked my suddenly dry lips. "Huh?"

"Let me explain." He hummed softly, deep in his throat. His gaze lingered on my cleavage showing at the top of my neckline. "On the night of a full moon, yes, your scent will call out to any man. But when you come into contact with a male who is an Elf our scent reacts to yours. What I'm feeling right now, you will feel. So much more, too. Neither of us will be able to say no." He leaned down, pressing his forehead to mine. "It won't be either of us doing the seducing, it'll be the magic."

I blinked. Sniffed. "I don't smell anything."

"I do. It's coming."

I stared at his plush mouth. The mouth I had always wanted to kiss. "Are you mad at me?"

"I would have preferred to wait until after your Blood Tree, but it's close enough."

"Just two days."

"Thank the heavens." He groaned quietly, tilting his head and placing his mouth against my ear. His sweet breath heated my flesh. "Here it comes. Are you ready?"

I smirked, using the phrase he always used. "You already know the answer."

# CHAPTER 7

A rush of magic jarred my senses, jolting my body in heady urgency. I inhaled a deep breath and held it in. It was strong. I could taste it on my tongue. This wasn't a scent like cinnamon or ginger. It was the scent of power and strength charging toward me, a sizzle on the air that had my back arching and my breasts pressing against his warm chest.

It was his unique scent. All Julius. All *original* Elf.

His mouth was on mine as my eyes closed in pure need. I moaned against my mate's mouth, his lips like a treasure of granted wishes. His hungry growl only fueled my flooding desire for him. Our lips parted, rubbing against each other's, and his tongue touched mine.

"Julius," I whispered. My hands lifted to thread through his soft hair. It was so thick, my fists clenched on the strands, holding on tight as he lifted me straight off my feet. Our tongues collided in a battle of insistence, neither of us giving up the fight to be closer. We wouldn't give up until *all* of our demands were met, our wait so long to be together.

He walked on strong legs to his massive bed, holding me in his arms and kissing my mouth again. And again. The hard brush of his flexing muscles against mine had my body rubbing against his, needing to press all of myself to him. His lips left mine for a heartbeat when his knees bumped the mattress, his words guttural. "Get rid of the bag."

It dropped on the floor with a thump.

He chuckled quietly, his dark carnal eyes finding mine. "Eager, are you?"

There was no shame in my game. "I want you naked. Like, right now."

His grin increased, and he tossed me onto his bed. I bounced but choked on a laugh as he grabbed my ankles, pulling my feet to the edge. He yanked my shoes and socks off, each one tossed carelessly over his shoulder. He wiggled his white eyebrows. "Ladies first, my mate."

I pouted. "Please take your shirt off for me?" *Before I jump on you and rip it off.*

His head teetered back and forth in thought. In a swift motion, his shirt was lying on the floor next to my bag. All that gorgeous tan flesh stared me in the face. His muscles rippled as he crawled onto the bed directly on top of me.

My hands smacked down on his biceps. I squeezed and dug my fingernails in, wanting him even closer to me. My words were breathless. "No wonder Mom told you to keep your clothes on at all times."

His eyes scanned my face. "So you like?"

"Hell. Yes."

"Good. It's my turn to stare." His fingers dipped under the hem of my shirt.

My eyes widened in shock when not only was my t-shirt gone in less than a second but so was my bra. I choked, "Had much experience with that?"

He was an intelligent man. He didn't respond.

Besides, his hooded gaze told me he thoroughly enjoyed what he viewed.

I poked his shoulder. "Don't drool on me."

His lips twitched. "A little bit of spit never hurts." My brows furrowed in confusion, but he just winked and tilted his head down to my chest. He whispered against my pebbled nipple, "You'll figure it out later, my Kenna."

A deep as hell groan left my lips, his tongue grazing my right nipple. Sinful. He was sinful as he switched back and forth from each breast, sucking and devouring me into a heated frenzy. I lifted my hips, grinding my core against his hard cock. My panties were soaked, his heat and mine matching in intensity. "Lower. I want your mouth *lower*."

He slid his hand between our bodies and cupped my crotch. "Do you mean here?"

"You know I do."

He hummed quietly, gradually pulling my zipper down. "Are you sure?"

I wiggled under him, staring up into his eyes, his scent digging deeper into my senses. "Quit teasing me."

His lips lifted, and he kissed my neck gently. "I'm teasing myself, too."

I groaned. "Well, stop. Teasing isn't nice or hasn't anyone ever told you that before?"

"I'm sadistic. What can I say?"

To hell with this. I shoved my hands down and yanked my pants over my hips. My mate snickered quietly, watching as I struggled to remove my pants and panties under the press of his body. My eyes narrowed. "If you don't help me, your pants won't be coming off either."

His brows raised, but damn if his hands didn't start assisting me. Black eyes roamed my naked flesh, the gleam in his gaze sinful. "In the future, any time you want to order me to remove your clothing, I'll be more than happy to contribute to the effort."

I smiled, showing all my teeth. "I thought you might see it that way." I pointed at his pants. "Off. Now."

Ripping fabric tore through the air, and pieces of his pants littered the bed.

I blinked. "That's one way to do it."

He grunted and shoved my knees apart. "Time to lick that lovely pussy, my mate."

My brows flew up at his gruff words, but my eyes quickly closed when his lips landed on my intimate folds. I'd had barely any time to even look at his cock, but I didn't give a damn. "Fuck. Lick all you want."

He bit my inner thigh, then his tongue was working a magic that was purely my mate in action. Diligent. Determined. On a damn mission. No argument left my lips, only my quiet demands mixed with moans of gratefulness. He lapped at my wetness as if it were his favorite savory treat, and tortured me as he twirled his tongue around my throbbing clit. His long years of life had taught him well. Two of his fingers slipped inside me, and I nosedived right into a blissful world he had created.

I came hard against his tongue, my body trembling beneath his.

He growled, kissing my clit one last time before rising over me. "You taste as sweet as I always imagined."

I repeatedly blinked into his gaze, trying to form a coherent thought. My mouth opened, but no words spewed forth. I hummed instead. That, I could manage right now.

His lips curved, and he kissed my left temple. He leaned to the side and grabbed a condom from his nightstand drawer. His lips twitched as I eyed the package, watching as he rolled it on his impressive cock. "Don't worry. It's new. Not expired."

I huffed and spread my legs wider as he settled between my thighs. His heat warmed me further, small beads of sweat already forming on my brow. "I like a man who's prepared."

"You like this man, you mean."

I ran a finger over his right eyebrow, my words quiet. "Only you."

His eyes met mine and held. "Only you."

My mate pressed his hips forward, his scent increasing in power and strength, a completion on the horizon to the magic holding us prisoner. I bit my lower lip as his cock stretched me full; the pinch of pain, as he passed my virginal barrier, was nothing compared to the rightness when he was fully inside me.

With his hips flush with mine, he breathed heavily. "I've waited eons for this."

I brushed my lips against his. "My mate."

"My mate." And he kissed me, the most tantalizing kiss. His hips pulled back, only to push forward again. His thrusts were gentle, caring for my tender flesh. "Does this hurt?"

"No," I moaned, running my hands down his flexing back muscles. "It's perfect."

Our rhythm stayed steady as we made love to one another. His body undulated against mine with each pump of his hips, his dark eyes staring down into mine with such adoration. I never stopped touching him, my fingers on a journey to discover every part of my mate. When I lifted my hips to his, meeting each of his thrusts, he groaned softly and teased me with his lips, brushing them over mine. Our climaxes came, just as I always knew they would, at the same time. Together, we soared into pleasured filled stars, our bodies joined as one.

The power chaining us together from the full moon dissipated, leaving us breathless and damp. Our chests rubbed against the other's as we tried to find air. Julius lifted his head from my left shoulder, his cheeks pinked from exertion. He raised one white brow. "It's gone."

I smiled. "It is."

He dipped his head and brushed his nose against mine. “Ready for round two?”

“Yes.” I patted his bare right hip. “And three. And four.”

“That’s my girl.”

# CHAPTER 8

Mom asked in irritation, "Where are you going now?"

"Didn't you want me to pick up your old Blood Tree cloak from the cleaners?" I grabbed my keys, my body still pleasantly sore from my all-nighter with Julius. And Mom didn't even have a clue. She had been sleeping soundly when I snuck back inside the lake house this morning. "You said I needed to pick it up at three o'clock today."

She rubbed her forehead and rolled her eyes. "*Five*, Kenna. Not three."

"Oh." I peered around our house. There was nothing to do, and I was bored. I shrugged. "I'll stop by the diner and grab an earlier dinner."

Mom dug cash from her wallet. College kids are epically broke. I wasn't any different. She waved the bills at me. "Pick me up ice cream on your way home."

Money always came with a price. I snatched the generous amount of green in front of me. "Will do."

She cleared her throat, staring pointedly. "I want my change back."

I scratched at my left arm. "I need gas."

She stared, but eventually nodded. "Fine. Just don't forget my ice cream." Her hips shimmied then. "And don't forget, we've got that movie marathon tonight."

My chuckle was deep. "Please. Don't wave those hips like that again."

Her nose lifted into the air. "Darling, I look as young as you."

That was a fact. It didn't change anything, though. "You're my *mom*. No. Hip. Shaking."

Before I strolled out the front door, she shook them one last time.

I slapped Jerry's shoulder as I sat down next to him on a barstool. "Back in town for a while?"

"Only for a few days this time. There's a freshman showing potential for the Majors." He wiped his fingers free of barbecue sauce. His baby back ribs looked tasty. "So what's new with you?"

I lifted a finger to hold off his question, and then hollered, "Hey, Mack! I'll have what Jerry's eating."

"You're changing it up." Mack tipped his head to me. "Full or half rack?"

"Just half. I'm having ice cream later."

His crooked teeth gleamed as he smiled. "You and your mom binge watching again?"

I winked. "You know it." It was a tradition on Friday nights. Ever since we stopped moving everywhere, we tried to make an effort to spend time together. Even if my Blood Tree were tomorrow, it wouldn't stop our pre-weekend ritual. "Do you want to know what we're watching this time?"

He snorted. "Not really."

I shrugged and turned my attention back to Jerry. "Anyway…what did you say?"

Jerry shook his head, used to my ways. "Anything new?"

I tapped my fingers on the bar, my words blunt. "Julius and I finally did the deed."

"Holy shit." He sat back on his chair, his grin wicked. "About damn time."

I stole a fry from his plate. "Yeah, I know."

Jerry's grin gradually faded. His black brows furrowed, and he cleared his throat. His words were hesitant. "Is there…uh…anything you want to talk about? Do you have any questions about your *encounter* that—"

I slapped a hand over his mouth. "You can stop.

It was fine." I grinned and removed my hand from his face. "It was better than fine, actually."

"Good." He cleared his throat again, definitely uncomfortable with his offer of help. He slapped my back. Twice. Like a guy coming off a baseball field who had just hit a home run. "That's good."

I snickered. "You suck at this stuff."

His cheeks actually flushed. First time for everything. "I know. I'm working on it." He stretched his shoulders and relaxed on his chair. His dark eyes met mine, and the confident and cocky man was back. "How the hell did you get that prude to give in?"

"He's not a prude." No way in hell was he a prude. He had proved that last night. "Let's just say I surprised him…and a full moon may have worked its magic."

He stared. Eyed me. Then tipped his head back and laughed.

I grinned. Jerry had a nice laugh—which was rare to hear.

"So a little voodoo action?"

"Something like that."

He shrugged his left shoulder. "Hey, whatever works."

I winked. "Exactly."

## SCARLETT DAWN

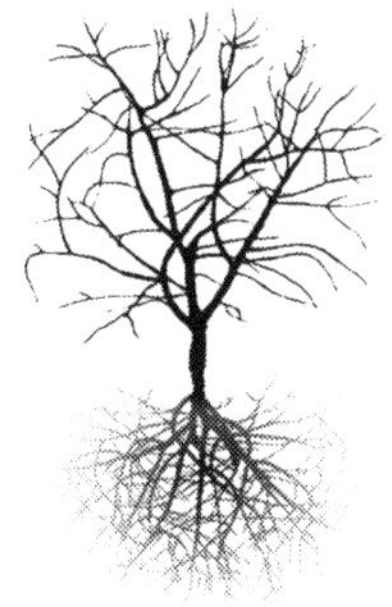

Jerry held the glass door open for me. "I'll see you around."

"Yep. Later-later." I stepped outside the diner, still wiping barbecue sauce from my mouth. I glanced at my watch. "Shit. I'm late." It was a half-hour past the time I was supposed to be at the cleaners. I nibbled on my bottom lip. Jerry and I had chatted too long. Mom was going to kill me. "I probably won't make it there in time before they close."

"Where?" His brows dipped low over his eyes. "Do you need help with something?"

I grabbed my key from my pocket and rushed to my car down the street. I shouted over my shoulder, "No help needed. I'll either get there in time or I won't."

He waved farewell, but ordered loudly, "Wear your seatbelt if you're going to speed!"

I grinned and slammed my car door shut. I was definitely going to break a few laws to get there in time. I buckled in, started my car, and shot out into traffic.

Three stoplights ran and twenty miles per hour

over the speed limit—the entire way there—I made it. Just as they were starting to lock the door. I rushed out of my car and banged on the glass door.

They had mercy on my poor soul. I shoved the gown into my large purse, paid them a little extra—thank you, Mom—and happily walked outside.

Only to have brutal arms grab me from behind.

My mouth opened to yell, but a sweaty palm landed over it in the fading light. I dug my feet into the ground and shoved my shoulders forward, but the man holding me captive drug me easily into the dark alleyway next to the cleaners.

I bit down into his palm and tasted blood. He grunted behind me. Panic had me kicking backward in self-preservation, and I connected with his kneecap. A sickening crunch rent the cooling air as his knee snapped backward. He shouted in agony and his arms loosened around my torso.

I shoved back as hard as I could with my elbows.

He lost his footing, wobbling on one leg.

And fell backward.

*Ting.*

Such an innocent sound.

It was the slightest vibration from the dumpster.

Where his head hit.

Poised on the balls of my feet to run, I stalled.

The stranger wasn't moving. At all.

Dark liquid pooled around his head onto the asphalt.

My adrenaline pumped for a whole different reason.

I kicked an empty soda can aside and dropped to my knees next to him. Uncaring if it was too hard, I whacked his face. "Wake up!" The blood pouring from his head started to soak into my jeans, the warmth of it making my stomach roll. I smacked him again. "Hey, asshole! Wake up!"

No movement.

"Oh, God. Oh, God." I leaned down and placed my ear to his mouth. "Fucking shit!"

He wasn't breathing.

I felt for a pulse.

*Nothing.*

"This can't happen. This can't happen." I jumped to my feet, determined that this man wasn't going to die. In the dark shadows on the other side of the dumpster, there was a back door to the cleaners. They had to be in there still. One of them could know CPR. I shoved forward, digging out my cell phone, preparing to call 911. Eyes on my phone, I grabbed the door handle. Thank God, it turned; it wasn't locked. With blood covering my hands and clothes, I stepped inside, my mouth open to scream for help.

But I froze solid.

Inside the back of the cleaners…

Well, it wasn't the cleaners.

Forty sets of eyes stared back at me. Forty people. The room I was in was dark, quietly lit by sconces on the walls. It was a massive room with couches and televisions on the walls.

It reminded me of the grand hall of the Light Elves.

But every person—except one in the right corner—had black hair. *All of them.* With *black* hair.

I had…just walked through the front door of the Dark Elves realm. I glanced at the door I still had ahold of. In the shadows, I hadn't been able to tell. I hadn't even been *thinking*.

The door was black wood. Oh… "Shit."

I blinked at it, and then took two steps backward.

I shut the door in front of me.

The traffic on the street was the only noise.

I stared at the closed door.

Then glanced at the dead man on the ground.

It only took a second before my feet were peddling to the street. I *ran*. I ran until I arrived at my car. My seatbelt was an afterthought as I sped away.

I went to a cheap motel, too afraid to go home.

To face my mom.

I eventually left her a message far into the night, "Mom, I'll see you tomorrow at the Blood Tree. I love you."

# CHAPTER 9

## *Age 20*

My eyes were bloodshot. I had a hangover from the booze I had stolen from a homeless man. I might even have bugs in my hair from the disgusting sheets I had slept on.

I had killed a man.

Happy birthday to me.

And I'd had to turn my phone off earlier.

The constant ringing was driving me crazy.

My mom was calling.

Julius was calling.

Susan was calling.

Hell, even Randor tried to call.

I sat in my car all day long, parked next to the lake house. All I had been told was I needed to be near a wooded area before the sun set. The Blood Tree would call me and lead me to my destination. The

Light Elves informed the Dark Elves—and vice versa—on the twentieth birthday of any Elf child. They would be there. Light and Dark. Both halves together for the decision.

I rested my head back and stared at the trees in front of my car. The sun was lowering closer to the horizon. My peaceful time was almost up. I could feel it resonating in my bones. Tonight would be interesting—and not in a pleasing way.

Just as the glare of the sun touched the top of the tree line, I stepped out of my car. I adjusted the silver hooded robe I wore. My feet were bare as ordered. With the top of my head covered with the hood, I stepped onto the grass and marched into the brush. There was no escaping destiny. A person merely had to face it straight on, instead of being blindsided by it.

I swiped my perspiring hands on my robe…and it came as the sun hit the horizon.

*My call.*

It was a charge to my blood, a pull in my veins. All I had to do was put one foot in front of the other. They knew where to lead to me. My flesh vibrated with a hum of electricity.

*My energy.*

What made an Elf immortal.

I ran my fingers through the air, each flick of a digit sparking a new current of pleasure-filled pressure through my system. My naked toes curled into the ground with each step, a pulse resonating deep inside the earth and tickling my tiny toes.

It was the best walk of my life.

And the worst.

Dread filled my belly. I was walking straight for the smallest dust storm possible, except it was black and white dust that swirled around each other. A small tornado of power.

*My destiny.*

With my eyes glued to the revolving magical storm, I clenched my fists and readied myself. I could do this. I could do this. Either way the Blood Tree decided, I was my own person. That would never change. And neither would the fact Julius was my mate—only one per immortal…forever.

Bits of black and white dust brushed my face the closer I drew. I blinked against the sparking charge that pelted my exposed flesh. It didn't hurt, but it wasn't pleasant, either. It was raw energy pulling me in.

I sucked in a harsh breath and crossed my arms, my feet skidding across the grass. There was no turning back now, the trees surrounding shaking with the force. The power had ahold of me. I closed my eyes as the energy storm swallowed me whole.

Then silence.

There was no wind. My cloak no longer fluttered.

There was no grass. My feet rested on a cold, hard ground.

I opened one eye, and then the other. Both widened.

I stood inside a room filled with Elves. And one hell of a huge tree in the center.

On the right, the Light Elves stood silently on a curving staircase all the way to the top.

On the left, the Dark Elves stood quietly on an identical staircase all the way up.

The right side had light shining down on them from an unknown source, their white hooded cloaks glowing with pureness. While the left stood in shadows from the tree, their black cloaks obscuring even their features. I couldn't see the top of the balcony on the Dark side—it was pitch black up there—but I could see Julius sitting on a chair at the top, the farthest Light Elf away from me. It was least powerful to the most powerful. A foot of distance separated him and Samuel, a railing set on each side, with a drop to the floor between them. Always separated.

I squinted, trying to see the most powerful of the Dark side. But it was too…dark.

My mom stood on the ground level with me. She was posed right next to the tree, wearing her white cloak. Her chest lowered in relief at the sight of me. Her grin would have lit my soul if I weren't so frightened. She gestured for me to come forward.

I lowered my arms to my sides, counted to ten in my head, and then walked directly in front of the Blood Tree. My eyes flicked up. What I had initially thought were leaves on the branches were actually green birds. Small birds all staring down at me as if they wanted to peck my eyes out. I shivered and hurried to peer away, my attention on my mother.

Her hood was far over her forehead, but her green eyes held mine. Her voice was strong and proud as she stated loudly, "Today, my daughter, Kenna Julius, mate to Julius, receives her immortality." *And designation.* The sleeve of her robe hung in a sweeping arc as she raised her arm and pointed to the ceremonial knife on the table next to her. "Kenna, if you would, please?"

I swallowed down bile and picked up the knife.

I knew this part.

I placed the tip of it to my left index finger and pressed. A small pool of blood formed on my finger around the blade. I sat the sharp object back onto the table. My eyes stared at the deep grooves of bark on the Blood Tree.

I inhaled. Exhaled.

And placed my bleeding finger against the tree.

The power that jarred my system sent me crashing to my knees. I threw both hands down to the ground to stop from completely falling on my face.

My limbs shook with raw energy.

Caws of birds filled the air, so loud it was near deafening.

I lifted my head. The tree and birds…were black.

I groaned and closed my eyes. "Mom, I'm so sorry."

She grabbed my wrist and jerked me to my feet. The birds quieted, but their black wings still beat the air. "This can't be right." She shook her head. "You've experienced none of the warning signs."

I pulled my arm back. My words were quiet. "I have."

"*Damn, this is bad,*" a male whispered on the right.

Mom's eyes rounded. "What have you done?"

Her head jerked up to look at Julius. "What has *he* done…"

I shook my head, not looking anywhere near my mate. "It's not his fault."

"Did you have sex with him?"

"Mom."

Her voice quieted to a peculiar calm. "Answer the question."

I closed my eyes against the onslaught. "Yes."

"Have you been to the Dark realm?"

I opened my eyes and stared straight into hers. "Yes."

Her nostrils flared, her tone whisper soft. "Have you killed someone?"

"Yes."

The quiet that descended on the Elves was immense.

"When did this happen?" Julius's voice boomed throughout the room. His tone was so frightening the birds froze in place. "Tell me now, Kenna."

I ground my jaw together and lifted my gaze. My mate was standing and squeezing the railing in a white-knuckled grip. His hood had fallen back and his normally pristine white hair was a chaotic mess all over his head. His cheeks were rosy red and his lips were formed into a thin line.

"I'm so sorry," I whispered.

"Now, Kenna!"

"Last night!" I shouted, throwing my arms wide. "A would-be rapist pulled me into an alley. I fought him off and he hit his head. It was an *accident*. I went for help, but I ended up in the Dark realm."

His blazing eyes held mine for so long.

I wasn't sure he was even breathing.

"I'm sorry," I whispered again.

My chest constricted as he turned.

And placed his back to me.

"Julius?"

He dropped his head and placed his forehead onto his right palm.

"Julius…"

My mate didn't move. Didn't speak.

"*Asshole*," Mom muttered under her breath. Her gaze darted back to mine. She stared at whatever expression I was wearing. "None of that. Not right now."

I sucked in a harsh lung full and blinked until my eyes no longer burned with tears.

Mom was still in shock, but she gestured to the left side of the room. She choked, "Go find your place."

Keeping my mouth shut, I nodded my head.

My bare feet were chilled on the ground, and as I trekked closer to the Dark Elves, my entire body was freezing. It was fear that gripped me hard, unknowing these people, the new family I was to enter. I stepped next to the first Elf on the ground level. The magic didn't stop me, so I kept moving, passing person after person.

The power of the Blood Tree would stop me when my magic level was lower than someone in line.

The tips of my toes touched the stairs. I lifted one foot after another, climbing the curving staircase. When I was halfway up, I no longer watched the Dark Elves faces. Each one was pissed when I passed them by.

Murmurs from the Light and Dark stilted the air when I reached the balcony. The Elves were seated up here, so I kept my head down, watching where I stepped in the darkness. Closer and closer, I drew to the end of the line. Until my head bashed into an invisible barrier.

I halted and lifted a hand. I pressed against the air, and I could go no further.

I was directly next to the original Dark Elf.

His second in command, sitting next to him growled a nasty curse. "Samuel, this is bullshit. I am one of the ten you created. It's not possible for a twenty-year-old to be more powerful than I am."

A hush fell on the room. I continued to stare at my toes peeking out underneath my cloak.

The man directly next to me, Samuel, cleared his throat, and then he stated evenly, "The Blood Tree doesn't lie, Valkor. She now sits next to me."

My eyes widened, and I jerked my head to the side. "Jerry?" My mouth bobbed seeing my friend. "What the fuck are…"

His black brows lifted. "You were saying?"

Oh. My teeth clicked as I shut my mouth. "Really? You spied on me that entire time?" Dark Elf. Scheming and manipulative.

His lips curved into a cruel smile. "I would watch over any of mine."

I snorted. "I was supposed to be a Light Elf."

"That was a wish." He gestured to the seat next to him. The one Valkor grudgingly vacated. "This is your reality." His head tilted to my mate, who was standing against the railing splitting us apart. Staring silently. "And he *is* an asshole. Your mother was right—even if for different reasons."

My lips pinched. I turned my attention to my mate.

Narrowed onyx eyes lifted from Samuel.

His gaze found mine.

Until he turned and walked away.

# CHAPTER 10

I glared at Jerry…Samuel. "Where are we going?"

"To your house so you can change into normal clothes." The original Dark Elf glanced away from the road and eyed my features. "It's your first night as an immortal. You need to feed."

My nose scrunched. "Where do we do that? A prison?"

His lips twitched, and he turned his attention back to his driving. Of my car. "While that is quite entertaining, we won't be having a felon party." He shrugged a shoulder. "I thought I would start you slow. We'll go to the city park."

"There are only drug dealers and…" I snapped my mouth shut.

"I think you understand."

"Yeah, we're going hunting for scum."

"That's all a matter of perspective. I'm sure you've known people in your life who have had a respectable job but have been malicious underneath their pleasant mask." A particular high school math teacher flashed through my mind. He turned the heater on low, warmth rushing around my cool bare feet. "Not all drug dealers are terrible. Some deal medicine to the homeless when they can't afford medical care costs."

I lifted a doubtful brow.

Samuel chuckled quietly. "You'll understand better when we arrive at the park."

I tapped my fingers on my knees and changed the subject. "So...how long have you been spying on me?"

"More than awhile." He shrugged, not apologizing for his behavior. "Though it was much easier when your mother put down permanent roots."

"Our chance encounter at the diner?"

"Not so chance."

I rolled my eyes. "Why didn't you just tell me who you were?"

His dark eyes flicked to mine. I stared. It dawned on me that Julius and he had the same black color. He lifted a black brow. "Would you have stayed around to chat if I had?"

"Good point." I jerked my attention away from him. "How else did you invade my privacy?"

His own fingers tapped on the steering wheel. "I pretty much know everything there is to know about you. I had my men dig a little when I realized you existed, and then I took over from there."

"You really didn't answer my question."

He smiled, staring at the road. "No, I didn't."

"Do you plan to?"

"Probably not tonight."

"You didn't stalk outside my bedroom window, did you?"

"Only once. Just to verify it was you." He paused. "You were sleeping. That's all."

"You know those little warning bells that ding in your subconscious when something's not right?"

"Yes."

"*Ding. Ding. Ding.*"

Samuel grinned and laughed. He still had a nice laugh; that part wasn't faked. "I assure you, Kenna, I have done nothing distasteful."

I snorted. "I suppose that's a matter of perspective, too."

His smile was broad, creasing his cheeks. "Indeed."

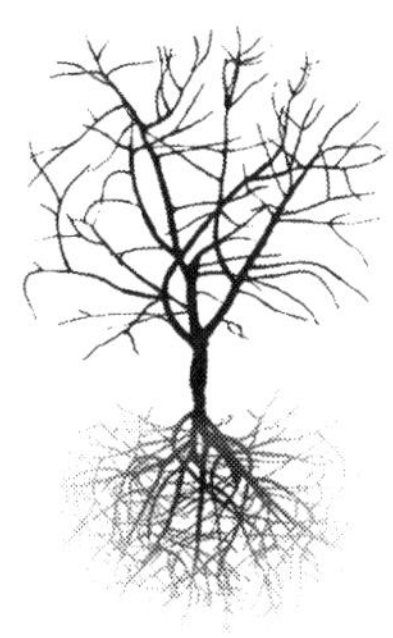

"Mom's not home," I grumbled. Her car wasn't in the driveway. "I won't take long to change."

His forehead crinkled, and he picked at his cloak. "Mind if I change in the bathroom?"

My tone was dry. "Let me guess. You already know where it is?"

Samuel winked. "That's a trick question. You have three bathrooms. One in your bedroom. One in your mother's room. And one next to the laundry room."

I slammed the door but bent and peered through the window. "Get out, smartass."

He grabbed his bag from the backseat of the car and followed me inside. No directions were needed. The Dark Elf headed straight for the bathroom next to the laundry room.

I jumped into the shower real quick. Dirt covered my feet and twigs stuck in my hair from traipsing through the forest. Plus, I needed a moment of solitude to process my new life.

As a damn Dark Elf.

Exiting from the shower, I quickly toweled off and changed. I tugged my hair up into a ponytail. Stared at myself in the mirror. I wasn't sure what an Elf wore to feed. My sweatshirt and yoga pants would have to do. I did make sure to tie my tennis shoes in double knots, just in case any drug dealers got the idea in their head to chase me down. You know, for *feeding* on them.

I grabbed a pair of scissors and stuffed them into my right pocket.

A little protection wouldn't hurt. It wasn't like I owned a gun or anything.

I walked into the living room and stopped cold. Blinked.

Samuel sat on the love seat on my right.

My mom sat on the couch on my left.

Both looked like figurines they were so still, their eyes averted from one another.

I raised my brows. "You two will learn to get along with each other."

Mom snorted.

Samuel grunted.

My eyes lifted to the ceiling and I sighed. "The Light and Dark aren't that different."

In a flash, both sets of eyes swung to me.

"Both feed off humans."

As one, they turned their attention away from me, averting their eyes once more.

Mom snorted.

Samuel grunted.

"Well, this is fun."

Snort. Grunt. In unison, this time.

I chuckled quietly. "Okay, that was enough time spent together for the first evening." I waved a hand at Samuel. "Let's go feed on some drug dealers."

Mom looked at him then. If glares were blades, his flesh would be bloody.

Samuel drove my car again. Demanded to. It gave me time to think anyway.

"Do I have to call you sir?" I asked as we stepped out of my car.

He shut the driver's side door, meeting me on the sidewalk. "For now? Yes."

"Like, in private too?"

"You can call me Samuel when there are no other Elves nearby."

"That'll work, I guess." I shoved my hands into my pockets, peering out into the night. "Where do we start?"

"That's easy." He placed his hand on my back and pushed me forward into the grass. "Close your eyes and concentrate on the energy in the earth."

I closed my eyes. "Do I always have to stand on soil to do this?"

"No. It'll become easier as time goes by. You'll eventually be able to do it from an airplane."

"Okay." I tilted my head to the side and tried to remember how the ground had tickled my toes during the Blood Tree call. That had been massive amounts of energy. "Can I take from the earth?"

Quick and short. "No. Never."

"Why?"

"It's too pure. Even for a Light Elf." He paused. "It could kill you."

My eyes snapped open. "So there is a way for an immortal to die."

"The only way. And it's suicide."

I shifted on my left hip. "Do many Elves take that way out?"

"Only a handful of the Dark have."

"And the Light?"

"Twice as many."

My brows furrowed. "Do you suppose that's because the world's been going to shit?"

The original chuckled. "The Light aren't that innocent, Kenna."

"Then why double the numbers?"

"It's a long story from a long time ago. It was a clusterfuck of miscommunication."

I slid my finger across my throat. "Why can't we die if our heads are cut off?"

"They can't be cut off." He flicked a finger against his neck. "Once you're immortal, nothing can penetrate our skin."

My eyes shot wide. "Seriously? I didn't know that."

He nodded and tapped his right foot. "But it's best to not be captured by anyone. There are other holes on the female and male bodies. It's hell if someone shoves a grenade down your throat…or stuffs it up somewhere else. The healing process for wounds like that takes months."

My mouth bobbed, and I choked on the words. "Have you had that happen before?"

"I'm old. I've had many unpleasant experiences."

I stared, and then turned my back to him and closed my eyes again. "I think we should focus."

He snickered. "I would agree." He waited a long moment. "Find the energy."

It was easily found. I wiggled my shoulders as it ran like fingers on the underside of my feet. "What do I do now?"

"Search for the voids in the power."

I clenched my fingers into fists, pushing farther and farther into the earth's power. It traveled out from me, and I could see the landscape without opening my eyes. Grid lines of green spanned the lawn. The trees were green fireworks shooting from the ground. Wooden park benches were dark brown and charred. Trashcans were purple and solid. The sidewalk was red checkers.

I breathed, "Wow."

"Found them?"

"No. Not yet." I kept my eyes closed and turned in a circle. I paused in Samuel's direction. Where he should be standing there were squiggly lines of silver shooting far into the sky. "You're not a void."

"Nope. All Elves appear silver in color."

I kept turning until I paused. My brows twitched, and I leaned forward. I squeezed my closed eyes tighter.

In the distance, two hundred yards away, there were holes in my vision.

It was nothing but black.

"Got 'em." I shoved a finger in front of me.

"How many?"

"Three."

"Open your eyes. Let's head over there."

With reluctance, my regular vision returned as I opened them. "I like it the other way."

He shrugged, walking in the direction I had pointed. "Some Elves prefer it that way. You'll learn to control it. In a few months, you won't have to close your eyes to concentrate. You're powerful so it'll come quicker than most."

We threaded through trees, marching on twigs and leaves. Human voices eventually carried to my ears. There were three different people talking. Two men and one woman.

"The voids are humans, huh?"

"That would be correct." He lifted his finger to his lips, indicating I needed to be quiet. He stopped our progress and whispered, "Can you feel your hunger?"

"Um, no."

He tapped on my forehead. "Up here. Not in your stomach."

I stared. "Uh…hold on. Let me check." My brows furrowed. "*How* exactly do I check?"

"Do you have a headache?"

"A little one."

He grinned. "That's your hunger. Elves are never ill."

My eyes widened. “Damn, that’s cool.”

“Do you want to relieve that ‘headache’?”

“I wouldn’t mind. It’s annoying me.”

“Focus on it. Once you find that pounding, become that beat.”

“Become the beat.”

“Yes, pour all of your being into the music thumping inside your mind.”

I stared at the ground. My head really started to hurt as I focused on that annoying ticking inside my head, my headache growing even further. I didn’t let go of it, though. I kept pushing it, striving to enhance the beat. I blinked and shoved a hand over my mouth to stifle my scream. On the ground, where I was gazing… my feet had disappeared.

Wait. I patted at my body because it was no longer visible. “Holy shitballs.”

“Shh,” Samuel hushed. But I could no longer see him either. He was invisible, too. “Grab onto the back of my shirt so you don’t bump into me. As I said, you’ll be able to see other Elves when your eyes are open, using the earth’s power, but you can’t do that now. The humans can still hear you, so you need to stay silent.”

I waved my left hand in front of me. And smacked Samuel straight in the face by the feel of it. “Sorry.” Though he did deserve it for deceiving me for so long. I patted at what felt like his shoulder until he turned and let me grab the back of his shirt. “How do I know which one to feed on?” I knew feeding on the light energy would make a Dark Elf vomit, and I somehow doubted anything that spewed from my body would be invisible like me.

"That's the easy part. You'll be able to tell which is more light than dark in a human when you're near them."

"Okay, lead me to the feast."

"Just stay with me. No matter what I do. And don't make a sound."

I nodded as we walked.

I pulled the scissors from my pocket.

Samuel stopped so suddenly, I slammed against his back. He hissed, "What the hell are you doing?"

"I'm following you. Like you said to do."

"No! With those scissors?"

"Oh. I brought them with me for protection."

Quiet.

I couldn't see the man, but I knew he was still there since I had ahold of him.

"What?"

The unmistakable sound of a bullet being chambered clicked in front of me. His tone was hoarse. "If you want to protect yourself, at least bring a weapon that won't make the bad guy laugh at you."

I blinked. "No scissors then?"

"I. Have. A. Gun."

I slipped the sharp cutter back into my pocket. "Okay, no scissors."

"Good fucking god," Samuel muttered, and then we were moving again. "Your mother babied you."

"She didn't want me to be Dark."

"And look where that got you. Right into my hands."

"Shut up. I want to eat some humans." I stuttered to a stop. "That came out wrong."

"Shh…" He didn't say another word as we crept up on the three unsuspecting individuals.

Instinct had me shoving at his back toward the woman.

The one buying the drugs.

Not the two men haggling her to pay a higher price.

Samuel headed straight for her.

My mouth slammed shut when…he walked right through her. My grip on his shirt was almost lost, but I held on tight. I closed my eyes as he pulled me through, too.

A creeping jolt of black electricity zapped my veins, and I was instantly more awake. I could run a hundred miles without stopping. I could build a house from the trees nearby—with my bare hands.

I was *alive.*

Samuel grabbed my shoulders as I stood between the three talking humans. On silent feet, he guided me back into the tree line. Within seconds, my invisibility wore off, my headache gone.

With wide eyes, I jumped in place. I had *so* much energy. "Can we do that again?"

# CHAPTER 11

I walked to my front door with a bounce in my step. Cycles of vitality rotated in my veins in a constant loop. I had never felt this wonderful in my life. It was hard to keep from laughing I was so energized. I grinned at Samuel, stating, "You don't have to walk me to my door. I've got my key."

His black brows were deep over his eyes. "I think I do."

"Why?"

"Because your mom's not alone. I'm pretty sure they're waiting for us."

My head snapped back to my home. "Who's in there?"

"An asshole by the power signature."

I walked faster. My mate was here. "Just him?"

"And your mom."

I shoved the front door open, my chest heaving. My gaze scanned the living room.

He was here. Sitting on the love seat. "Julius?"

My mate pointed to the couch. "Sit next to your mother, please."

Samuel shut the door behind him as he walked inside. "Julius. It's always a pleasure."

"Cut the shit out, Samuel. We need to have a discussion."

"You mean you have demands."

Julius's nostrils flared. "If I had demands, you would know it." His onyx eyes flicked to mine. "Kenna, please. Take a seat by your mom while he and I talk."

I stood my ground, crossing my arms. Though I would try to be civil. "You were unkind today."

He ran his right hand through his white hair. "I didn't handle it well. I am sorry for that."

"I'm a Dark Elf."

"I know that," he griped in irritation.

"Do you hate me because of what I am?"

"Of course not." He shook his head and pointed to Samuel. "I hate that he *owns* you."

I stared. "Come again?"

"Samuel owns all the Dark Elves. They are his to protect. And his to discipline."

A buzzing started in my ears. "I think I will sit down." I walked without blinking until I sat directly next to my mother. Her thigh was warm and comforting against mine. I waved a hand between the two men. "Feel free. Chat away."

*Fix this, Julius.*

Samuel leaned back against the wall and stuffed his hands in his pockets, his dark eyes steadfast on my mate. His words were blunt. "Let's skip past all the sweet words that I'm sure you're about to say and get to the heart of the matter." One black brow lifted. "What kind of trade are you talking about? Please remember, she is the second most powerful Dark Elf in existence. She is a rarity for such a young age."

"I know damn well what she is," Julius snapped. But he leaned back in his chair, getting comfortable. I tried to ignore that they were talking about me as if I were a piece of cattle. If Julius could bargain for me… so be it. My mate shrugged one shoulder. "I'll allow you to have your holiday back."

My mom's mouth gaped open, but she quickly shut it. And then pretended to act as if it hadn't happened, placing her arm around my shoulders and resting her head against mine.

"My annual Dark celebration?" Samuel clarified.

"Yes."

He tapped his right foot. "What else?"

Julius ground his teeth together. "I'll give you that knife you've always wanted."

Samuel froze. "From the gladiator?"

"Yes."

Black brows lifted. "What else?"

Julius closed his eyes for a long moment, and when he opened them, his gaze was patient. "I'll give you fifty billion dollars."

My eyes damn near popped out of my head. *"What?"*

Julius just waved his hand at me, hushing me, his attention never leaving Samuel.

"Money's nice, and I'll take it," Samuel murmured. "But I know you can do better than that."

Julius kicked his feet out and folded his hands on his flat stomach. "Why don't you just tell me what it is that you want? This negotiation will go much faster if you do."

Samuel grinned. "I want half of her."

"Explain."

"You are her mate. I understand this. But she is my subject. I don't want to lose her."

"So your proposal would be?"

"Along with all that you have already offered, I propose that any of her teachings are done by me. If she gets into trouble, you and I will determine a suitable punishment. Her protection will be handled by the both of us. And her vote in any future decrees will always be Dark Elf. I want half of her. Half of her time. You won't be able to stash her away as an Outsider." His lips curved up at the edges, a wicked smile. His tone turned whisper soft. "And you'll owe me a favor."

My mom gurgled deep in her throat.

Julius just stared. "But she is mine."

"And she is mine. Only in a different way."

Julius's forehead crinkled, his words gentle. "You're not physically interested in her—"

"Hell no," Samuel hissed, completely affronted. "Do you accept my proposal or not?"

My mate's lips thinned. "You've never asked for a favor before."

"You will give it to me if you want her."

Julius gazed to the side of the room. When his

words came, they were barely audible. "You have a deal."

Instant. "I'll expect payment of all of the tangible goods within the week." Samuel pushed off the wall. His dark eyes met mine. "I'll pick you up tomorrow at noon for more training."

Struck mute, I merely blinked.

"Nod your head if you heard me."

I nodded.

"I'll see you at noon." He walked out the front door, gently shutting it behind him.

# CHAPTER 12

"What am I learning today?" I asked, watching the scenery pass by. Samuel was driving my car again. I was beginning to wonder if he even owned an actual car. "I have no idea where we are right now."

"I'm taking you to a vacant parking lot."

I peered straight at his profile. "Fun."

He snickered. "You need to be able to find a door to the Dark realm anytime you need it. A parking lot with nothing around is the perfect spot." Because I could never enter the Light realm again since the Blood Tree had declared me Dark.

I still stared. "I have to find a door out of nothing?"

"If you ever need an escape route from humans, you need to be able to do this."

I groaned and rested my head back. "We're going to be here all day."

"Maybe."

I groaned again.

His eyes flicked in my direction. "How did it go after I left last night?"

"Well, after you made my mate a poor man—"

"Fifty billion would hardly leave him destitute."

"Anyway, after your little chat, Julius sat there for fifteen minutes not saying anything. My mom and I didn't bug him. He didn't give off the vibe of wanting to chat, you know? When he got up, he mumbled something about a 'damn favor', kissed my cheek, and left."

Samuel's lips were trembling. "And your mom?"

"She poured herself a generous helping of vodka."

He busted up, laughing so hard I grabbed the wheel to keep us on the road. He knocked my hands away, still chuckling. "I would have loved to have seen his face."

"You two should go to counseling. Maybe if you did, you wouldn't hate each other. Talk through your issues and stuff."

"Please, tell him that. Then take a picture of his face afterward." He glanced at me. "I'll give you a million dollars if you do it."

My mouth hung open. "I will not. He's my mate. I won't embarrass him on purpose."

Samuel grunted. "Give it time."

"I won't."

"All couples have their ups and downs, including mates. And due to the fact we never die, Elves tend to take things to the extreme during those peaks and valleys." He snickered. "I remember this one time where—"

I yawned. Loud.

"What?"

"Anytime my mom starts with 'I remember this one time,' it ends up boring the shit out of me." I shook my head. "And she seems to forget that she's told me the same stories over and over again."

Samuel's smile was easy. "Good memories shouldn't be frowned upon."

"And…they still bore me."

His lips twitched. "Again, give it time." He turned the wheel, and we went over a curb. Right into a vacant parking lot. The original Dark Elf put my car into park. "We're here."

I grumbled as I shot out of my car, checking the tires. I pointed to entrance seven feet away. "That is where you should have turned in."

"Your car's fine. Besides, if I break it, I'll buy you a new one." He eyed my vehicle. "Actually, I may buy you a new one anyway. How old is this thing?"

I threw my hands up in the air. "Mom bought it for me for my high school graduation present. It's only two years old." I waggled my hands at the tires. "And that isn't the point. You need to respect other people's property."

"I do. When it's worth something."

I smacked his shoulder. But I couldn't help the laughter that bubble forth. "You are an ass."

"Yes, I am." He clapped his hands and walked away. I hurried to catch up. He opened his arms wide and spun in a slow circle. "Kenna, find the door."

I scanned our surroundings. "I know it should be here—since we're here—but I don't see anything." My eyes stung with the sun glaring on them. I lifted a hand to shade my gaze. "There's nothing here."

"Where did you find the previous door?"

"In an alleyway."

"Be more specific."

"Next to a dumpster."

"What had happened then?"

"You already know."

"Keep thinking, Kenna. What was different?"

I stopped turning in circles, running the images of that night through my mind. It wasn't pleasant.

Samuel sat down on the cracked concrete and crossed his legs. He leaned back on his muscular arms, cocked his head, and watched me work through it. "What. Is. Different?"

I wiped the small beads of sweat from my forehead. "There's not a dead man lying on the ground."

He smirked. "That's a good thing, but what else?"

"I had blood on me then." Maybe it had to do with the Blood Tree.

He shot that idea to hell, though, shaking his head. "We will be here all day if you think like that."

I glared at him for a moment but started walking in a circle around him as I kept working out the problem. "I was scared."

"Just because you're Dark, it doesn't mean all feelings associated with us are bad."

"The door was attached to a building, but there are no structures close to here."

His lips twitched. "You're getting warmer."

I stopped moving, my attention snapping to him. "Is this a trick?"

"What do you mean?"

"Like, you take me somewhere that I actually can't access the Dark realm." My eyes darted all around. "The Light Elves need a white love tree, which is usually associated with the forests. If the Dark Elves need a black wooden door, it would generally be associated with a building."

Black eyes twinkled up at me. "So what have you learned?"

"I'm right then?"

"You are. This was a trick training exercise."

I nibbled on my bottom lip. "The Light Elves are best protected near heavily wooded areas, whereas the Dark Elves are best protected in a large city."

Samuel nodded and stood to his feet. "Very good." He rustled the hair on top of my head. "Now let's go jump off some bridges."

"Huh?"

"You need to get used to jumping and falling. It can be frightening at first."

I stared. This *so* went against everything my mom had ever taught me. "I never thought I'd say this, but if you jump off the bridge first, I'll follow."

His eyes gleamed with excitement. "I know the perfect one. It's really high."

"Oh, joy. My leader is an adrenaline junkie."

He shrugged. "Maybe."

"Maybe, my ass."

# CHAPTER 13

Julius was sitting on my front porch when we pulled up into the driveway. I smiled and waved. His expression turned from storm clouds to a bright rainbow day in a heartbeat. He lifted from his perch and sauntered to my car.

I didn't give him a chance to open the door for me. I hopped out and jumped on him.

He caught me with one arm around my waist, a silly grin etching his features. "I missed you."

"Missed you more." I planted my lips right on his, not caring that Samuel was getting out of my car or that my mom was walking out the front door. Julius didn't seem to mind they were watching either, holding me even closer, and brushing his mouth against mine in a wicked embrace. I pulled back when his tongue slid into my mouth and grinned. "Hold that thought."

He lowered me to the ground and asked in a reasonably calm voice, "Is there a reason why the two of you are soaking wet?"

I cleared my throat, and then bounced where I stood. "We jumped off bridges."

My mom groaned and marched back inside, slamming the door after her.

Julius chuckled quietly, brushing a strand of my dark hair behind my ear. "I take it you had fun?"

"I did." I wiggled my brows. "And Samuel gave me a tour of the Dark realm."

Julius's nose crinkled. "I suppose you do need to go there occasionally."

"More than occasionally," Samuel interrupted, stepping beside us. "She will hold a position in the higher Dark ranks."

Julius's jaw clenched, but he nodded. "I expected as much."

I waved a hand between them, earning my mate's attention back. There was no need for hostility. "The Dark realm looks pretty much like the Light realm. Except the color schemes." My lips twitched. "As you can imagine, they're all darker hues."

"Yes, so I've heard." Julius kissed my forehead, bending to place his face in front of mine. "I have a surprise for you, my Kenna. Why don't you get changed so I can show it to you?"

I flicked a finger between the two originals. "No fighting while I'm inside?"

Both nodded their heads. *Very* slowly.

"No fighting. I'm serious." I waggled my finger at them as I walked to the front door. "If I hear one shout from the two of you, I won't do training for a month, and I won't accept visitors here."

Glares were their return answer.

"Good. Behave." I shut the door behind me.

My mom's tone was dry where she was peeking out the front window. "I can't believe you left those two alone."

I shrugged. "You'll keep an eye on them."

"I will definitely do that." She shimmied her hips, her eyes glued outside. "I am the best mom *ever.* Just remember that, my darling daughter."

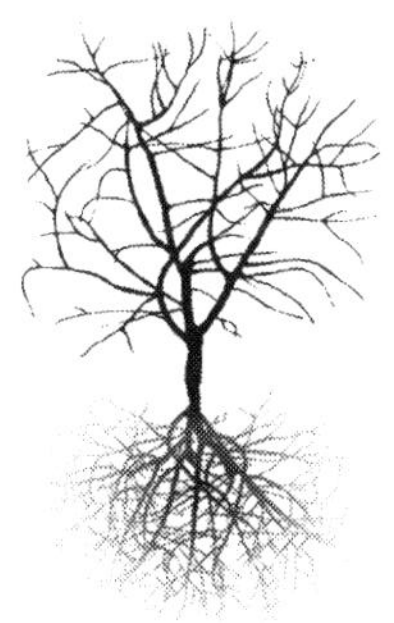

"This place is cool as hell," I muttered. My eyes peered everywhere as I dropped my overnight bag on the tiled floor. There were so many unique colored paintings hanging on the walls. "What's the name of this resort again?"

"Haven Resort." Julius stood behind me and wrapped his arms around my waist. "So you like it?"

"I love it and the lakefront outside." It reminded me of my monthly visits to the lake house with my mom. "It's perfect."

He twirled me around to face him. "There's plenty of trees nearby and tons of buildings."

I placed my arms around his neck, smiling up at him. "Safety first, huh?"

"Where you're concerned? Fuck yes."

I lifted on my tiptoes and pressed my lips to his, gifting him with a small taste of what was to come later tonight. Then I tipped my head to the empty receptionist's desk. "Where's the staff?"

"Mmm…there are none yet."

My brows snapped together. "What do you mean?"

"I mean, I haven't hired any yet."

"I need further clarification, my mate."

He grinned. "I bought this place. For you and me."

My jaw dropped and my arms tightened around his neck. "The resort is ours?"

Julius nodded. "We'll sleep in bed together every night, and it's close enough for you to still attend college." He sniffed, peering down his nose. "And see your mom whenever you want."

"But, what about the Light realm?"

"Randor will take over for me outside of working hours." He tipped his head to the grand entrance to the resort…our home. "And there's plenty of space for any Elves to stay the night here if they wish to speak with me then."

I rubbed my lips together. "Will Dark Elves be able to stay here, too? I may have the same issue eventually if Samuel has his way."

"Yes, the Dark Elves can stay here, too." He paused, his forehead wrinkling. "As long as they conduct themselves accordingly."

My smile was content, and I sighed. "You bought us a mixed family home."

He lifted one white brow, his lips twitching. "My mate is a Dark Elf."

I opened my eyes wide, gasping, "My mate is a Light Elf!"

Julius chuckled softly and lifted me into his arms. "And your mate's going to show you just what a Light Elf can do to a Dark Elf."

I hummed deep in my throat, kissing his right earlobe. "Promise?"

"Always." He strolled with me in his arms through the foyer. "But, first, I have to remember which bedroom is ours."

I snickered. "The one with the biggest bed."

"And a black, wooden closet door." He kissed my forehead. "Just for my mate."

"I don't deserve you."

"You can make it up to me…as soon as I find our damned bedroom."

I rested my head against his shoulder. "That's my man."

# JULIET'S STORY

# CHAPTER 1

### *Age 20*

I rubbed my tongue on the roof of my mouth. It tasted like ass. My eyes opened into the darkness, and I squinted and peered to the right. A vertical, outlined rectangle of shining light was all I could see—a closed door with a glow behind it. I blinked up at the ceiling inside the intimate room and groaned at the heavy beat of bass thumping outside of the room. I was at a sex club. "What the hell did I just do?"

A man snorted beside me. "Believe me, honey. I did most of the work."

My brows puckered, and I turned my head on the pillow it rested on. "Wonderful. I lost my virginity to a smartass."

His chuckle was quiet. "Yes, I do remember you shouting about how fine my ass—"

I slapped a hand over his mouth, those delicious,

wide lips that had caressed every hidden part of my body. "I'm drunk, but not that drunk. There's no need to quote me. I haven't forgotten." I pushed up on my elbows and held the thin sheet close to my bare chest. "How long did we sleep?"

"About an hour." He stretched in the darkness, the sheet pulling against my hold. His taut muscled legs rubbed against mine, our bare feet still touching.

"Good. Susan should still be here." I needed a ride to the closest tree line. Partying in downtown on the night of my Blood Tree had been such a great idea…until I wound up in a dark room with a stranger and shoving our tongues down each other's throats. Then groping other body parts in more intimate areas. I brushed my white hair out of my eyes. "What's your name anyway?"

"It's—"

"Juliet!" Susan hollered, throwing open the door. A blast of light flooded the interior of the room from outside, the music pulsing even more fiercely against my pounding head. I raised my hand to shade my eyes. My companion for this night's outings—a celebration for me becoming an official Light Elf—stopped dead in her tracks. Her eyes widened as she glanced back and forth between the man lying beside me and myself.

I hugged the sheet closer to my chest. "Yes, I finally lost it. You don't need to stare."

She gurgled deep in her throat, unblinking at my Cherry Popper.

"What?"

She pointed.

The man moved then, growling so quietly I could barely hear him. "You're fucking Light?"

My attention shot to the side, watching as he sat up beside me. My jaw slowly went slack, hanging open. This…wasn't good. With eyes scanning his features to memory, praying I never saw him again, I sputtered, "Fuck. You're Dark."

He ran his fingers through his jet-black hair. His eyes damn near glowed in the light from outside, reflecting with a fire meant to spear straight through me. He grabbed my right bicep, my arm so much smaller than his gripping palm. I froze as he ran his thumb over the small tattoo of a pink star on my shoulder.

His question was soft. Menacing. "Did you do this on purpose?"

I yanked my arm out of his grip and rolled out of bed. In a hurry, I snatched my clothing off the floor, ignoring how his penetrating eyes ran over my body with rage. "Hell no. I wouldn't be with a Dark if he were the last man—"

"Well, I'm sure as fuck not the last man on earth and we still fucked!" He jumped out of bed, throwing the sheet to the side in fury. Susan quickly averted her stunned gaze to the floor as we both began to dress in heated silence. He jammed his legs into his boxer briefs and glared at me. "You need to leave out the back door. I can't have anyone see you go downstairs with me."

I snarled, jerking my gaze to my friend. "I blame this on you. You knew there were going to be Dark Elves here! But no! We *had* to come to this happening joint." I clipped my bra together and mimicked her. "*Come on, Juliet! You'll have so much fun. I promise.*" I bared my teeth.

With her gaze still fast on the floor, she choked. "Technically, you did—"

"Shut up!" I shouted, waving my hands at the Dark stranger. "This was not fun."

He stalled as he buttoned his jeans. "Excuse me?"

"Dammit, you know what I mean." I shoved my sweater over my head, pushing my arms through the right holes. "I'll leave out the back door. No problem there."

He pulled his own shirt over his head. "And you'll keep your mouth shut?"

"Fuck yes, I will."

"Mom, I slept with a Dark." The words just spewed out of my mouth, no filter at all. I blinked back the tears burning my eyes. I had crept behind her like a thief in the night, too frightened to speak. I watched her work on the dishes for five minutes, and still hadn't come up with a game plan except the truth. I could barely breathe my chest was so constricted. But I needed a "mother's" advice. I hoped she would be a mother this time. "I had too much to drink…and it just happened."

My mom's hard gaze narrowed as she sat down the cup she was cleaning. "One more time?"

"I slept with a Dark," I whispered. My chin trembled and my fists clenched. I prepared myself for an ass-chewing.

She turned to face me fully inside one of the communal kitchens in the Light realm. Light Elves still roamed the hallways even though it was close to midnight, their quiet, respectful chatter barely heard. My mom tightened her apron around her thin waist, keeping her hands busy. "When?"

"Tonight."

Her nose crinkled in distaste. "His name?"

I sputtered, "I don't know."

My mom's blink was gradual, her tone gentle as a whisper. "A stranger?"

"It was an accident! The room was dark. I just went in there to get away from the crowd."

Tightening. Her. Apron. "Did you use protection?"

My mouth snapped shut, and my gaze drifted over her left shoulder. Stayed there.

"What the hell, Juliet!"

I threw my hands into the air. "I know." My head shook. "What do I do?"

My mom snarled. "You sure as hell don't tell your father."

"Mom." I shook my hands at her. "What do I do?"

I wished I was anywhere but here as the silence extended.

Eventually, my nerves tingled in unease.

She stood still for so long, a Light Elf came inside the kitchen, took one look at us, and left without a comment. And still, she was mute. Just staring hard into my eyes.

When she finally spoke, her words were quiet. Simply spoken. "You leave the Light Realm."

My eyes grew wide and burned more fiercely. "No."

"Juliet, you don't know if you're pregnant or not." Her forehead crinkled, creating tiny wrinkles on her young face. "You'll have to become an Outsider until you know for sure."

"No."

She peered away from me and clasped her hands together at her waist. "Yes."

I tilted to the side, trying to catch her eyes.

But she wouldn't look at me.

My heart hammered inside my chest and swelled in a painful ache. "You're disowning me."

Her throat moved, swallowing. "If you're pregnant, with a possibility of it being Dark…"

The sweltering tears I had been holding back spilled over my eyes, pouring down my flushed cheeks. "I don't want to leave you." I coughed on my words, the clog in my throat too constricting. "Or Dad. I want to stay here." They had never won a parent of the year award, that was for damn sure, but they were still my parents.

Her attention never moved from her blind stare to the side. No words came forth.

"Mom…"

Her nostrils flared.

"Mom!"

Her gray gaze snapped to mine.

I froze.

"Leave, Juliet."

I opened my mouth. Shut it. I pled, "Please don't make me be an Outsider." I shook my head in disbelief. How the hell was this even happening? She had been so proud of me at my Blood Tree. "I can't live with the humans. I don't have any money—"

"You do. You have a bank account."

"There's hardly anything in there."

"It's enough to get you started."

"Mom…please don't do this." I grabbed for her hand.

She jerked away from my touch like I had scalded her. "Leave." She pointed a sharp finger at the door. "And I'll pray that you're not pregnant."

I took a faltering step backward, toward the exit. "I'm sorry! Please—"

She turned her back to me and crossed her arms. "Not sorrier than I am."

# CHAPTER 2

Susan shifted from one foot to the other, her struggle to hold my boxes making her arms shake. "Are you going to open the door?"

My hands were free so I placed them on my hips.

And I stared. Not saying a word.

Shit had gone down. Major life changing shit.

My eyes were bloodshot. My bank account was already dangerously low from renting an apartment—on my own. The bottom of my shoes were covered in mud thanks to the heavy rain. And my family had disowned me. Susan deserved the burn in her muscles from holding too much, just a little portion of my agony. I merely stared as she held all my possessions in her arms. Only when she wobbled, almost dropping my clothes hanging over her arm, did I unlock my door.

She sighed and darted inside. "When are you going to forgive me?"

"When you pay me back." I entered my 'home' and slammed my door behind me.

Susan carefully placed my items on the furnished couch. "I can pay you."

I shook my head. "I'm not talking about money." She was older than I was with much more cash than my meager savings. "One day, you will owe me a favor."

Her lips thinned, her white brows drawn together. "One day?"

"Yes. One day."

"When will that be?"

I grimaced, peering around my tiny one bedroom apartment. "The hell if I know."

"So…you're going to be upset with me for a long time."

"Upset doesn't do my feelings justice."

"Angry?"

"Higher."

"Pissed?"

I waved my right hand up.

"Furious?"

I growled, "I'm devastated, Susan! *Devastated*."

Her white brows lifted in surprise. "The chances that you're pregnant are slim. You'll be back in the Light Realm with your family in no time."

My eyes narrowed with fresh burning tears and my voice was gruff. "I'll never go back to them."

She stared, eyeing my features. "What?"

"My family has left me out to dry." The red mark was long gone from my left cheek, but my dad's parting comments would always haunt me. My mom had been right. I never should have told him. "You didn't hear what my dad said. I'll never go back to them."

She popped her knuckles. "Never is a long time for an immortal, Juliet."

I scanned my sparse apartment once more. "Damn if I already don't know that." I jerked my head at the door. "Get out of my place. I'll call you when it's time to pay up."

Susan held still. "Let me help you. If you're serious, you'll need—"

"I'm not a charity case. I'll get a job and finish college like any normal human does."

"But—"

I opened my door. "I don't want you here. Please go."

Her feet faltered, but she strode forward. Her voice was stronger as she passed by me. "This wasn't all my fault. You are the one who slept with a Dark Elf."

I closed my door on her face.

And my lips twitched.

I knew it wasn't her fault. My anger had subsided on that issue.

But I now had a favor I could call in.

My attention turned back to my new life, my apartment.

A favor was always handy to have in an unknown future.

# BLOOD TREE SILVER EDITION

The timer on the oven blared. I shoved up from my chair and jerked the knob to the side, cutting off the heinous noise. I made myself trudge to the bathroom, one foot moving in front of the other, the walk of a dreaded immortal lifetime.

Two months and my period hadn't come.

I braced my right hand on the door frame and peered down to the pregnancy test on my bathroom counter. I couldn't take my eyes away from it. The answer was plainly visible. I didn't need to stare as I was, but my attention didn't waver away from the truth.

I placed my free hand on my lower stomach.

I tried to swallow. My throat was too dry and the saliva pooled at the back of my throat choking me. A single tear trailed down my cheek. More came, flooding down and dripping off my chin. The cooling drops splattered against my collarbone, dampening my heated flesh. I didn't take my hand away from the door frame to wipe them away. I would fall if I let go.

It was official, my life was over.

My youth was gone.

I was twenty-years-old, and I needed to call an OBGYN to make a well-check appointment.

I was a kid having a kid.

I was going to be a mom.

And I was going to do it alone. As it needed to be.

# CHAPTER 3

The chipper receptionist in the emergency room smiled as I walked through the door. "How can I help you today?"

"Get me a damn doctor," I hissed, holding my belly heavy with child. "I'm in labor."

That stupid smile stayed right in place. "What is your doctor's name? I'll have a nurse call to inform him or her."

I ground my teeth as another contraction zeroed in like a missile. My right hand slammed down on the countertop. "Dr. Who-Gives-A-Fuck-Right-Now."

My normal OBGYN was in Hawaii on vacation, and in my current condition, I didn't feel the need to tell the smiling human. I snapped my fingers at the wheelchair behind her. "I need to sit."

I wondered if her smile was constructed from plastic surgery when it merely lifted bigger while she stood and rolled the wheelchair around her desk to me. "What would your name be?"

"Juliet Julius," I mumbled, sitting heavily on the chair. "I need drugs."

She leaned down and winked at me. "We have the best painkillers at this facility."

Okay. Maybe she was using them, too. It would explain a lot. "Wheel me toward them." But the phone on her desk began to ring, and my attention honed in on her. I grabbed her left wrist, and growled, "Don't even think about it."

With a delicate twist of her arm, she removed my restraining hold with no issue. "You are my number one priority right now. Don't you worry about a thing."

I snorted but gripped the armrests. She pushed my wheelchair at a fast clip down a hallway, making my damp hair ruffle back in a swift breeze. Definitely not painkillers then. Maybe some form of speed. "Don't tip me."

"Never. I've been doing this a long time." She hummed to herself, jerking us around a corner and heading toward a set of white double doors. "Ms. Julius, I must say, your hair is positively glowing it's so beautiful."

I grunted. "Drugs."

"Drugs it is." She opened the white doors and pushed me into another waiting area. There were three nurses standing behind a counter, all busy with charts or paperwork. And wearing those same ridiculous smiles on their faces while they worked.

"Lots of drugs," I muttered and rubbed my temples. "And get me a doctor who doesn't look like they just graduated high school or sound like they sucked on helium."

The receptionist chuckled. "I know just the doctor for you."

"You need to push now, Juliet," the ugliest human imaginable demanded in a deep baritone. No smiles there. His face was crinkled with a lifetime of scowls and his hands were marred with age spots. This doctor was perfect. The speed-loving receptionist had come through. "One. Two. Three. Push!"

"Am I doing this right?" I spoke through gritted teeth, bearing down and pushing as ordered. A nurse on either side of me held my limp knees back to my chest. "I can't feel a damn thing."

Drugs were *good.*

"That's perfect," Doc answered. "Give me another one."

I inhaled heavily and groaned as I pushed with all my might. Still, I felt no pain. Panting, I muttered, "Do you see anything yet? What color is the hair?"

Doc blinked up at me.

Like I had just asked the funniest question.

I waggled a finger between my legs. "Watch what's going on down there."

His bushy brows puckered, and he peered back to his work. "I'm assuming you mean the hair on your baby's head, correct?"

My white brows shot straight to my hairline. "Good God, don't grow a humorous bone now."

He chuckled quietly. "A little humor takes the edge off."

"Tequila takes the edge off. Not a doctor cracking a joke while he's hands deep in my vagina."

The nurse on my right coughed hard…and her lips trembled.

"Not you, too."

"Oh no, miss," she stated respectfully. "I learned the first hour not to get on your bad side."

Damn straight she did. "Do I push again or what?"

"Just a second," Doc murmured, bending at the waist for a better view of my exposed flesh. "I think I see the baby's head." His lips curved into a private smile. "Lots of hair, actually."

"What color—"

"Push!" he cut me off. "Now, Juliet."

Inhaling through my nose, I squeezed my stomach as hard as I could. And kept pushing.

I *needed* to see my baby *now.*

"That's excellent," Doc stated. "Give me another one like that."

I growled with the effort to shove a child out of my *babymaker.*

The resulting sensation was too peculiar for words.

My stomach was full, and then suddenly it wasn't.

Round one moment and flat in the next.

Just…gone.

As my chest heaved in pants, the doctor ordered, "Stop pushing." His bushy brows lifted and he actually smiled. "It's a girl."

I blinked and gazed at his forehead.

My mind went blank.

No questions formed past my lips.

I had a daughter. A girl.

*My* baby was here.

My little baby. Mine to hold.

*Mine* to protect.

And then she squalled so loudly, I started grinning, too. "Can I hold her?"

The nurses were helping the doctor, but one wrapped her in a blanket and placed *my* child on my chest. My arms instantly cocooned the tiny bundle. She hardly weighed anything. So small and breakable. A precious gift given to me from the most unlikely of individuals—a Dark Elf.

I laughed quietly as my daughter's eyes opened, her chin quivering. "You're my Kenna." I lifted my head from the pillow and kissed her forehead where wisps of her hair were sticking out from under the edge of the blanket. "Black hair and all."

# CHAPTER 4

## *Age 26*

I peered down at my darling daughter and straightened my blue wig, careful not to show my white hair. Humans tended to comment on the light hue. The less attention I drew to us the better. It was odd that humans didn't look twice at my blazing wig, but with my natural hair color, they stared.

Humans. They were weird.

Such a short lifespan, and yet they continually filled their daily lives with unhealthy habits.

Smoking. Crazy driving. Disgusting foods. And laziness.

I had them pegged down pretty well. It was one of the reasons why I was climbing the corporate ladder in marketing. All I did was flash ideas of the exact opposite of what humans were, what they wanted to be—instead of how they truly lived their lives—and it was the next big pitch in my company.

Show the humans what they think they are. Easy.

Bam. Paycheck.

My daughter stared at me with pleading eyes. "Mommy, can't you come in with me today?"

"I took off yesterday for your first day of school." I brushed a strand of her jet-black hair behind her right ear. "I can't miss another day of work."

"*Please.*"

"I can't, Kenna. I'm sorry."

"Pretty please?" Her green eyes flicked to one of her classmates as she was being escorted into the elementary school…by her dad. I closed my identical green eyes as she bounced on the tip of her toes and pointed. "See? Other parents are going in!"

I sighed, my chest heaving. Damn humans. I took my daughter's hand and stated, "I'll take you inside and drop you off at your classroom. But only if you list the rules."

She scratched at her right arm and pulled me forward to the entrance. "Okay! Never open a black—"

"Shh. Tell me in a whisper."

She puckered her tiny lips and breathed quietly. "Never open a black wooden door. Never kill anyone—even accidentally. Never have sex before…" Her head tipped up and her lips pinched, staring straight into my gaze. "Mommy, what's sex?"

I coughed as a teacher glanced at us. "We can talk about this later, darling. When you're much older. That's good enough for now." My feet hadn't stopped moving forward, keeping up with my child's quick pace. When we arrived at her classroom, the scent of crayons and erasers tickled my nose. I knelt down on one knee in front of her. "I'll be here to pick you up. Don't leave with anyone else."

She shook her head. "Strangers are bad."

I nodded. "Exactly. What do you do if someone tries to take you?"

"Scream."

"What else?"

Her grin turned devious. "Do whatever it takes to run away."

"Do you remember where I said to hit?"

"In the privates."

"Very good." I covertly flicked a glare at her teacher gawking at us. "And what about policemen?"

"Kick them too if they try to steal me."

I kissed her forehead. "You are my angel."

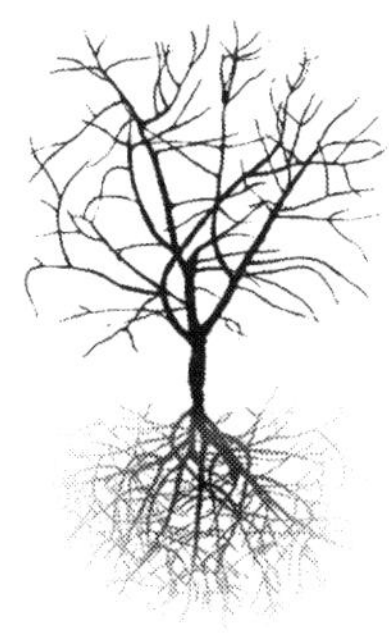

I watched my daughter as we walked through the supermarket. I *always* watched my daughter.

The signs were there in her simplest actions.

Kenna smiled up at me as she picked up an orange and placed it with the apples.

I shook my head. "No, darling. That creates extra work for the employees."

She eyed the out-of-place orange. "But the colors are pretty like that."

I cleared my throat. "Kenna."

"Hmm?"

"Kenna."

Innocent eyes peered up at me.

"What did I tell you about lying?"

Her small shoulders hunched in. "Fine." She picked up the orange and placed it in its rightful place. "But it's funny to watch the other people see it."

My daughter loved chaos. Even if she didn't notice it. "It may be funny, but it's still not nice to do."

She strolled along beside me, her head no taller than the middle of our shopping cart. "My teacher said it isn't nice to hit policemen."

"*And your teacher's an idiot*," I mumbled under my breath, too quiet for her to hear. Dark Elves loved to take jobs as policemen. There was evil prime for the taking with that profession. I cleared my throat and stated primly, "I'm your mother. Who do you think is right?"

Her eyes widened. She held my gaze as if I were a superhero, and my heart ached with utter love for my child. "You are. Of course!"

"That's right." I pulled her in close to my side, and silently wondered how long I had before she realized moms weren't always right. That we didn't have all the answers. That a parent can make a mistake. But, dammit, I would protect her until the end of time. "I love you, darling."

"I love you too, Mommy."

# CHAPTER 5

## *Age 34*

*Bang.*

The screen door slammed behind my daughter as she stormed out into the backyard. But the pounding on the front door was even more jarring. I kept my bracing hands on the vibrating wooden frame and breathed a sigh of relief.

Good God. Kenna had actually mentioned calling the cops. The police coming were the exact reason I had ordered her to leave in the first place. Our nosy neighbor across the street would have made sure of that. The two human idiots ramming their fists against my front door were nothing compared to the Dark Elves who would be here soon—and these fools lived a street over.

*Had I not impressed upon her enough cops were no good?*

Apparently, we would need to have another talk.

I removed my hands from the front door,

adjusted my pink wig, and jerked the door open wide. The scent of sour beer wafted inside off the two dumbass humans standing on my front porch, the ominous clouds overhead an unneeded warning that a storm was brewing. I waved a hand in front of my face to clear away the stench. "Are you the morons who fucked up my car?"

"I'm sorry, lady," Dumbass One slurred. He scratched at his receding brown hairline. "I can pay for it."

I was sure he could. Their house was three times the size of mine. "Just your insurance information will do."

Dumbass Two cocked her head, her smile sloppy-stupid, a pretty Belle used to getting what she wanted. She waved a pointed finger in the air. "About that. We would prefer not to have our insurance company know about this little…incident." She hefted her purse up from her hip and swayed side-to-side, bumping Dumbass One. "We'll write you a check instead."

My brows lifted. Too many DUIs, I would bet. "Look, I know where you live." I hooked a thumb over my shoulder in the direction of their place. "Why don't we take care of this another day—" I shut my mouth and groaned quietly. The unmistakable blare of sirens flittered in the air. "Shit."

Dumbass One and Dumbass Two glanced at each other, their eyelids fluttering. If I had the ability to smell fear, they would reek of it.

I glanced at the clock. I didn't have much time before sunset. The full moon would be here soon. The police would be mine to handle, not the two drunks on my porch. I would give them my statement as fast as I could, and then lock myself down in the basement—far away from any male Elf's sensitive nose. With my plan firmly in place, I grabbed my purse off the floor where I had dropped it and charged straight between the two morons. I closed my door behind me and made my way to the sidewalk edge.

I waited for the police to stop their cruiser in front of my wrecked car that was now my own personal debris mound.

Two men stepped out.

One was a blond human.

One was a black-haired Dark Elf.

My upper lip curled *seeing* his power signature hovering taller than mine in the air. He was more powerful than I was, but that wasn't saying much. During my Blood Tree, I had literally been blocked from passing the first Light Elf. I had been the lowest in ranking. My power kept me immortal but didn't do much else. "Gentlemen."

Both tipped their heads to me in greeting.

The Dark Elf eyed my slight cleavage showing at the neckline of my tank top. "Ma'am."

I realized right then he wasn't using his power. He was using his regular vision—no different than a human. The Dark Elf must be young. He didn't know I wasn't human. I blinked and quickly altered my expression, plastering on a fake as hell smile. "I'm so happy you two made it here. Those two drunks hit my car." I lifted my eyes to the sky and sighed noisily in feigned exasperation. "And I have a teleconference I'm scheduled for in a few minutes inside my home. Will you take my statement real quick? I have all my information in my purse."

The human cop nodded and began taking my statement.

The Dark Elf immediately veered to the two idiots still standing on my porch. It didn't surprise me. The Dark were always drawn to chaos.

I kept an eye on him and watched his every action.

Chaos chases trouble and often escalates it.

I really didn't want a fight breaking out on my front lawn.

Done giving my recount of my car being totaled, I placed my insurance card and license back into my purse and glanced at the human policeman. "Is that all you need from me?"

"That would be all, Miss. We'll get those two out of your hair quickly."

"Much appreciated." I turned and walked across my yard, but I stopped solid. Another cruiser was pulling up in front of my house. I peered back to the cop I had been speaking to. "Why are there more of you here?"

The Dark Elf answered for him. "These two have felony warrants out. We're taking extra precautions with them."

I held back my laugh. Bullshit that was his plan. I eyed the two handcuffed and sitting on my pristine green grass. Dumbass One and Dumbass Two must have enough dark energy in them to feed plenty of Dark Elves. I rubbed at my forehead as the human policeman conveniently decided to take a walk down the street. He flashed five fingers to his partner and a warning glance, indicating he would be back in five minutes—a damn dirty cop. My attention turned to the two policemen exiting their vehicle and the plain-clothed man they generously opened the door for in the backseat.

The oxygen in my lungs disappeared. My feet wouldn't move. I stared, unblinking, at the man in expensive dark jeans and a simple white T-shirt that stretched over his honed muscles. My gaze ran over each of his features in rapid succession, like a speeding train derailing. Each symmetrical curve of his face I remembered as if it were yesterday, not almost fourteen years ago.

It was *him*. The man with no name.

Kenna's father.

All three men stopped in their tracks, halting at the edge of my property. Their eyes were honed on mine. They were seeing me, my power, as I was theirs. All of them were Dark Elves. And the plain clothed man, his power shot so far into the sky, it had to touch the heavens.

My mouth bobbed. "Fucking perfect." Kenna's dad was a high-ranking Dark Elf.

Her father's black brows snapped together as he scanned my face, but he quickly peered to the right to the setting sun, eyeing its quickening descent. The sun cast a succulent glow on the side of his tan face as his attention drifted back to mine. His words were a quiet drawl. "It's a little late for you to be out, don't you think?"

Perfect opportunity. I flicked a finger at my house and regulated my breathing. Hyperventilating wouldn't be wise right now, not when he didn't recognize me. "I was getting ready to go inside." I turned and stepped quickly around the handcuffed morons. "Have fun with those two. Make sure to drop them somewhere away from here."

The first Dark Elf on the scene was bewildered, his eyes snapping back and forth between us, clearly lost on the byplay. He *was* young. "I'm not sure what you're talking about, ma'am."

I snorted. "Open your damn eyes and *see*." I climbed the steps on my porch and safely entered my home. Breathing wasn't easy, but I concentrated on it, placing my back against the front door. I should have moved from this town a long time ago and not stayed where Kenna had been conceived. I tossed my purse onto the couch and banged my head back against the door three times. "Stupid. Stupid. Stupid."

*Tap. Tap. Tap.*

My eyes widened and my head slowly turned to the side.

*Tap. Tap. Tap.*

I grimaced and opened my front door.

He stood there. Silent.

My lips thinned. A breathless word escaped. "Yes?"

His head tipped to the side, and a loose lock of

black hair fell across his forehead. He ran his fingers through his hair, pushing it back…while he stared quietly at me, his dark eyes running over my features. My fists clenched when he lifted his left hand and ran his thumb over my right shoulder. "That's an interesting tattoo. I think I saw it once before."

Dammit it all to the Dark side. "I'm sure you're mistaken."

His lips curved into the smallest crooked grin. "I think not."

I stood mute…until I shook my head. This couldn't be happening. Not right now. "The sun's setting. You shouldn't be here."

He shrugged a shoulder and stepped past me into my home. "We still have a few minutes." He pulled the door out of my hold and shut it behind him, trapping us inside my house. His dark eyes instantly filled with fire and held me immobile. His rage hadn't abated in all the years since our encounter. "Let's chat before I need to leave."

# CHAPTER 6

I scanned my living room for any evidence of another person living here. I kept no pictures of us visible in the main room. Kenna's blue blanket was in the corner, but he wouldn't know it belonged to a thirteen-year-old. Though her luggage was still on the couch from our ruined trip to the cabin, it was plain red. Nothing screamed 'a teenager lives here.'

I snapped my gaze back to my intruder. "This is not smart." The power of the full moon would be rising in me soon. He wouldn't be able to say no. He wouldn't want to say no. And with one touch from him, I wouldn't be able to either. "You really need to leave."

He leaned toward me and delicately sniffed near the top of my head. His light cologne smelled of soap and leather, all male. The darkness of the room where we had met hadn't done him justice. He was deceptively unremarkable. It was as if magic hid his perfect features from first glance, but when you stopped to actually look at him…he was stunning. This man was the perfect predator hidden amongst the humans. His nostrils flared, and he closed his eyes.

He took a step back from me before lifting his eyelids. "It's nothing I can't handle right now. A few minutes won't hurt." He pivoted and stalked my living room in a slow glide, eyeing each piece of art hanging on my wall before moving on to every trinket sitting on the mantel. In the quiet surrounding us, his dark eyes flicked toward me. "This is your home?"

I crossed my arms. "It is."

A black brow lifted. "You're an Outsider?"

"I am." I lifted my chin. "What of it?"

His gaze skimmed over my features before he shrugged. He continued his perusal into my personal life, touching everything with a soft brush of his fingers. His words were offhand. "You're young to be an Outsider."

I snorted. "You have no clue how old I am."

His lips twitched and dark eyes found mine again. "The more powerful the Elf, the more obvious it is on another. It's in your power signature." He lifted a small stress ball from my bookshelf and flexed his fingers, fisting the small blue ball. "Didn't anyone teach you that? Or is Julius slacking in his duties?"

"Julius taught me fine." It was a small fib. I hadn't been in contact with the Light ruler since I had left the Light realm. All I had learned was from my time before when I lived there and being self-taught afterward. A few Light Elves had offered after I had left, sent by Julius's head of security, but I had turned them down. I had almost been showing my pregnancy at the time and didn't want any Elf around to know the truth. I wiggled my nose at him and pointed at the stress ball he continued to repeatedly squeeze. "This is enough chatting. You're going to blow soon."

He rubbed his lips together, his eyes not missing anything. He ignored my comment and continued with his questioning. "Did you ever tell anyone about us?"

My blink was slow. "Hell no."

He nodded. "As I guessed. I would have heard about it if you had." He stopped clutching the stress ball and tossed it from one hand to the other, playing catch with himself and standing clear across the room from me now. "Just so you know, I thought you were one of my normal women coming into the room that night. After you kissed me—"

"You kissed me first."

"—I realized you were inexperienced, not one of my regulars. But I still believed you to be Dark."

I stared. "Thanks." *Asshole.*

He shrugged. "It was your first time. You weren't completely terrible."

My brows lifted to my hairline. "It's time for you to go." I uncrossed my arms and gestured to my front door, lying to get the jerk out of my home. "The sun has set. I can see it in your face."

He tossed the ball from side-to-side. His tone was a calculating nuance, barely above a whisper. "Tell me. What do you see?"

*A handsome as fuck asshole.* I pointed to my lips. "Your mouth is turning white with tension."

His eyes danced between mine before he tilted his head back and laughed. And it was special. His hilarity was a site to behold. I doubted he laughed much. He shook his head at me, his dark eyes crinkled at the sides. "Would you like to tell me a different lie? You've been on a roll since I walked in here."

I snorted. "I hardly ever lie."

"So I'm just special?"

"You're special, all right."

His eyes crinkled further. "I detect sarcasm in your tone."

"Oh no. You're a special Elf I just love having in my private residence. You can come by anytime."

His crooked smile returned, so deceptively innocent. Predator. "I was already in your private residence once before. And I believe you came before me."

"Yes. I remember." I rolled my eyes and stared. He placed the stress ball back in its place perfectly, his movements concise, and then stuffed his hands into his pockets. He rocked back on his heels and popped his neck. "You really are showing signs now."

"I know." He shrugged a shoulder. "You're weak, though."

My words were dry. "For an intruder in my home, you just keep hitting me with the flattery. I don't know how much more I can stand. Really, you shouldn't be so sweet."

His lips twitched, his words simply asked. "Do you know how close you came that night to being buried alive?"

"I'm taking it, it was a close call?"

"About the same as now."

I crossed my arms again. "What's holding you back?"

"You're friends with Susan, and from what I understand, she's had the eye of Randor for some time now. She is under his protection. And by association, so are you."

The head of security for the Light. "I'm sure she would find that interesting." It was probably best not to tell him that I hadn't been friends with her since I left the Light realm.

"Will you tell her?"

I teetered my head back and forth in thought. "I don't think so. She can figure that out on her own." And when she did, Randor would have some explaining to do. Susan has had a crush on him since she was old enough to sit up straight. "It could be fun to watch play out."

"That it could." He cleared his throat and shook his head, running his fingers through his hair again. He stared at the ground and shoved his hands in his pockets once more. "It's time for me to leave."

"I've been saying that for a while now."

When he tipped his head up, peering at me from under his dark lashes, I held perfectly still. The heat that now burned in his eyes wasn't simmering hatred. It was something else entirely. A burn of desire aimed directly at me, his nostrils flaring as he scented the air. "The sun has completely set."

I didn't comment as I pressed my back against

the wall. I merely tilted my head to the front door, indicating he should take a hike—in a fucking hurry.

"The others are out there." He ground his teeth together, his muscles strained tight. "They're waiting just outside your door right now."

Okay, I had to speak up. Loudly. In the direction of my front door. "I'm not into group sex! Please go away." I jerked my head toward the door. "You too, tough man."

"I am tough." His tone was a low growl, his cheeks flushing with adrenaline as he stared. His nostrils flared and he closed his eyes slowly. When he spoke, his demand was as soft as a rose petal. "Go lock yourself up somewhere."

I didn't need to be told twice.

With his statue still form standing in my living room, I raced down the hallway, shouting over my shoulder, "Lock my damn door when you leave!" I slammed the basement door shut behind me, jumped down the stairs as fast as my feet would take me, and barricaded myself in the ancient wine cellar in the corner of the room. It was tiny, standing space only and reeked of mothballs. Ignoring the claustrophobia that immediately settled in the pit of my stomach, I pressed my ear against the door and breathed a small sigh of relief when I heard my front door hammer closed.

I still didn't exit. I would be here all night.

This was not the cabin retreat I'd had planned.

With my head resting back on an empty shelf, I groaned a half hour later when my cell rang in my pocket. Maneuvering wasn't easy, but I managed to pull it out. I didn't know the number on the screen, but I had known a phone call would be imminent. It was just a guess as to which Light Elf it would be. "Hello?"

"Still mad at me?"

My eyes closed. Speak of the devil. "Susan. What a surprise. How are you?"

"Oh, you know, dancing in the moonlight."

"Alone, I hope."

"For now." She was quiet over the line. "So…I have some news."

I snorted. "What would that be?"

"Randor texted me."

"And?"

"Apparently, an unknown black-haired Elf showed up in the Light realm tonight." She cleared her throat. "Know anything about that?"

I sighed. Kenna was now known to them. It wasn't in the ultimate plan of keeping her safe, but it had been needed. One evil against a lesser evil. I had picked and the consequences were here now. "She's okay?"

"She is," Susan answered instantly. "But you may want to brace yourself. I have more news."

My white brows furrowed. "What?"

She hesitated.

"What?"

"Your daughter found her mate."

I sucked in a harsh breath. "In the Light realm?" Oh God, this was *good* news. Maybe I had been wrong all along about my precious daughter and her predilection for chaos. "Why do you sound worried? This means she's a Light Elf."

Susan hummed. "Well, that is definitely in her favor now, and she did find the Light realm on her own." *Not really.* "But her mate…it's Julius."

I froze completely. "Huh?"

"Our leader. Julius. She mated with him."

"Uh…"

A passing beat of silence. "Juliet?"

"Uhm." *He's too powerful!*

"Breathe."

I inhaled heavily, then coughed on dust. Tiny particles of dirt rested on my tongue, and I swallowed them down on a scratchy throat, the sure burn not even noticed. I stared, blinking into the dark, not seeing a damn thing. "I'm calling in that favor you owe me."

Easy. "Name it."

*Kenna.*

"Watch over my daughter anytime she's in the Light realm. I don't want her getting too 'close' to Julius before her Blood Tree."

"You want me to friend her?"

I clarified, "*And* protect her."

She chuckled. "Done. But he won't touch her before her Blood Tree. He's a stronger man than that." She paused, clicking her tongue inside her mouth. The constant popping grated on my nerves. "So you're not mad at me anymore?"

"No. Your debt will be paid on her Blood Tree."

"Deal."

My thoughts swirled with worry, honed directly

on my daughter. But I asked absently, "Did you know the man I slept with?"

"You sure you want to know? You didn't ask then."

"I didn't think you knew him. You never said."

Her words were soft. "I do. I've seen him around a few times."

I closed my eyes. "What's his name?"

"Are you really sure you want to know?"

"Yes. Just tell me." My gut churned in unease, a sickly punch of dread creating small beads of sweat on my forehead.

She didn't stall. Blunt. "His name is Samuel."

My head dropped, and I hissed, "*Jesus.*"

"Close to but a wee bit darker."

Kenna's father was the original Dark Elf.

Their leader. The most powerful.

And scary as fuck.

My decision was so easy it was laughable. "I think I'm going to take a promotion I've been offered. We'll be moving soon."

We would keep moving. Kenna would hate it, but so be it. Her adolescent anger was nothing compared to saving her soul. Her father wouldn't catch us again from my own stupidity; his claws wouldn't be hooked into my daughter before her Blood Tree.

"My daughter *will* be a Light Elf. I swear it."

# CHAPTER 7

## *Age 36*

I glanced at my watch. This date was a bad idea, a complete step out of my comfort zone. Not to mention, this human would probably stick me with the check—not that this dingy, poorly lit restaurant would be expensive. "We're going to miss the movie if we don't hurry. The theater is clear across town." The romantic comedy feature would be the only highlight of my date night if this pathetic dinner were any indication. And I had been waiting for this movie for four months. "Maybe you can tell the waitress that you don't need that other beer you ordered?"

Jeremy leaned forward on his chair, resting his forearms on the table between us. His deep brown eyes ran over my bright orange wig, and then more gradually over my features. His soft Southern accent was an intimate rumble when he spoke. "I thought we could skip the movie."

*Oh, hell no.*

My lips curved into a polite smile. "I don't think so."

His head cocked. "Too soon?"

I couldn't stop the chuckle that escaped. "You tell me, Jeremy. How do you think our first date is going so far?"

He sat back on his chair and crossed his arms. Shrugged. "Not great, but not bad either."

"So…you think that's an indication for us to jump into bed together?"

"Honestly?"

"Of course."

A brown brow lifted. "I got the impression that's what you wanted when you asked me out." He waved a hand at the barely eaten entrees before us. "That's why I mentioned this horrible diner. It's only five minutes from my house, but it has a great selection of alcohol."

My lips pinched, and I quieted. My white brows puckered. "Did I seem that hard up?"

His right hand lifted, and teetered back and forth. "A little."

"Oh." I cleared my throat. "I am sorry for that. It wasn't my intention."

His resulting smile was easygoing. "Don't worry about it. It's good that we both know what the other wants now." A finger flick at me. "You wanted a companion for the night." His finger pointed to his chest. "I wanted a *companion* for the night." He laughed gently. "Perhaps we'll both get what we want by the end of the date with the confusion cleared up."

My own lips twitched. "You're really direct, aren't you?"

His grin increased. "Only to beautiful women. I know what I want when I see it."

The warmth in my cheeks burst into life, leaving me flushed. I glanced down and played with the napkin on my lap. I hadn't been complimented like that in… forever. Maybe this date wasn't such a bad idea. A small smile played on my lips as I raised my head, my mouth open to reciprocate his kindness.

But I froze.

Any thought of a pleasant evening was shoved aside with the arrival of one man.

My mouth snapped shut with a jarring click, and my eyes flew wide in shock. The beating of my heart pounded all the way into my head, booming a heinous rhythm behind my eyes. I placed my right hand on my forehead and used my fingers to rub it, pushing the dizziness aside. It wouldn't be enjoyable to regurgitate my atrocious dinner right now, so I swallowed down the bile that rose in the back of my throat.

Jeremy's brows snapped together, his eyes on mine, before he twisted around on his chair, following my frightened stare. When his gaze merely landed on a black cashmere sweater, his head tilted back to eye the intruder of our evening. "Can I help you?"

Samuel placed his right palm on Jeremy's shoulder. My stomach flinched, a whisper of Dark power charging the air, sizzling and electric—and cruel. Samuel's grip on my date tightened, his words crisp. "You can leave."

Jeremy's blue eyes glazed over. His frame swayed on his chair. He didn't peer away from Samuel, his regard caught on his trap of influence. Jeremy nodded with a jerk of his head. His tone was soft as if children were sleeping nearby and he was whispering into their dreams. "Yes, I will go."

"Now." Samuel smacked his shoulder. Twice. *Hard.* "And don't speak with Juliet again."

"I won't speak with Juliet again." My date stood from his chair on wobbly legs. He pivoted around Samuel and staggered straight to the door, bumping a few tables as he went. The other customers grabbed their teetering glasses and watched him leave, their scowls fully in place at the rudeness.

All while Samuel sat on my date's vacated chair, his dark eyes hard on mine.

Holy. Fuck.

The waitress stopped at our table, confusion clearly shadowing in her hazel eyes, the ice-cold mug of dark liquid in her right hand. "Um…did the other guy leave?"

"I'll take that," Samuel murmured. He raised his hand and took the beer from her, his gaze never leaving mine. "And I'll take the check for their dinner." He flicked his free hand at her. "You can go now."

She blinked, and then hurried away, her brown uniform shirt quickly disappearing.

Any remaining flush that might have pinked my cheeks was long gone. I stammered, "What are you doing here?"

Samuel took a sip of the beer, eying me over the

edge of the glass. "Remarkably, I'm here for the same reason your *companion* was." He wiped a bit of beer from the corner of his mouth. "He was an amusing fellow."

My eyebrows lowered. "You were spying on us?" I sat back on my chair and blinked. "And what do you mean you're here for the same reason?"

Samuel sat the beer down on the table and pushed Jeremy's plate aside. He placed his clasped hands on the table, those dark eyes of his filled with unsheathed rage, holding me perfectly still. "Would you like the long version or the short version?"

I couldn't breathe with him staring at me like that. "Uh."

Samuel smiled, baring his perfect white teeth. "I'll go with the long version."

I was pretty sure he wanted to tear me apart. "That'll do."

"You see, Juliet, you are a terrible liar. I knew something was off at your house, so I had my men look into you more. Your past was fuzzy with hardly any details, since you left the Light realm on the night of your Blood Tree."

I swallowed on a dry throat and gripped the edge of my chair, my fingernails digging into the hard metal on the side. "Okay. Your point?"

"My men mentioned one important clue to your odd behavior. You have a teenage daughter."

I stared. Tried to breathe.

His voice was a low growl. "*My* daughter."

Sweat beaded on my forehead. "I don't know what you—"

"Shut up, Juliet," he snapped. His thumbs tapped together, scanning my hooded gaze. "You can cut the bullshit. As soon as they told me she had black hair, I took over the investigation. I know she's mine. I ran a DNA test on her before your first move."

My mouth snapped shut, a fire erupting inside my gut. I slammed a hand down on the table and hissed, "How the fuck did you do that?" She was *mine* to protect. I couldn't have failed her.

"Do not take that tone with me," Samuel demanded, his jaw clenching. He unlinked his fingers and fisted his hands on the table. "You have no idea just how close you were to being eternally tortured at my hands. You're damn lucky that you're a wonderful mother to our child." His dark eyes flayed my flesh. "And you're young. It wasn't hard to figure out what you were doing hiding her from me."

"I was keeping her safe," I ground out between my teeth.

"You thought you were. Hence why you aren't nailed to my bedroom wall." He shook his head and pulled his hands into his lap, relaxing back onto his chair. "What you have yet to learn about our people is that nurture only goes so far. What an Elf is lies within the nature of the person. You can't stop an individual from being Light or Dark. It is who they are at conception."

I snorted. Glared. "She will be a Light Elf."

"That is doubtful. You're the weakest Light and

I'm the most powerful Dark. You're still young while I've been around since the Garden of Eden. Who do you think has the stronger genes?"

*He's wrong. She still has a chance.*

My lips pinched. "You still haven't explained how you ran the DNA test."

He hummed softly. "I snuck into your home a week after we spoke. I stole hair samples from her brush." His nostrils flared. "You moved soon after that. And you kept moving. Each time you picked a new place to hide, it took me a while to find you on my own. But each time, I did. I watched and evaluated, taking my time to resolve what to do with you."

My eyes flicked between his. I inhaled heavily and exhaled slowly. "And what did you decide?"

"That's why I'm here." He cracked his neck. "I have a deal to make with you."

Gradually, I crossed my arms. "And if I don't take it?"

His lips curved. "You'll be nailed to that wall I spoke of."

"Tell me what the damn deal is." I sighed in defeat.

"There are a few conditions." He shrugged a shoulder. "I can't change what has already been done. So going forward, one, you are a good mother so I won't interfere with what you're doing with Kenna—even though it won't help—as long as you stop running and hiding. I'll only enter her life under a false name and gradually get to know her and watch over her from afar. With the changes she's been through in the past few years, I think it would overload our daughter and confuse her further to know about me. *But only for right now.* After her Blood Tree, whether she turns out Light or Dark, you will tell her I'm her father. I want to be a part of her life."

My jaw clenched. "Do you know Julius is her mate? He won't like this."

"Yes, I know about Julius. And you won't tell him."

I closed my eyes for a few moments before opening them again and grabbed my glass of water. I took a large gulp to wet my dry throat. "What else?"

"Two, you will no longer allow another man into your bed."

I choked on the water, shoving the glass back onto the table. "Excuse me?"

He ignored my surprise, commenting easily, "That brings us to number three. You will be available to me for sex anytime I wish."

# CHAPTER 8

"I don't think I heard you correctly."

His smile was crooked and cruel. "Don't fret. You heard me just fine."

The waitress stopped at our table. I didn't look at her. My vision was honed on the Dark Elf directly in front of me—and on the words he had spoken. She glanced between us, noticing our silent exchange of a stare off before mutely placing the bill down in front of Samuel and scurrying off like a frightened deer.

When she was out of earshot, I muttered, "Are you out of your damn mind?" He was old. Perhaps insanity had finally taken hold—even though Elves were *supposed* to be immune to that. "Why in the world would you want to have private sex privileges with me?"

He tilted to the side and pulled his wallet out of his back pocket. It was the first time his eyes ventured away from mine. The original Dark Elf studied the bill as he said, "I thought I couldn't produce offspring. Kenna is my first child." He scratched his chin absently. "Forever is a long time to live without children."

My jaw went slack at his humbling honest confession.

*His first child?*

Damn. I was in serious trouble.

He placed a hundred dollar bill on the table and cleared his throat, putting his wallet away. Only then did his attention lift back to mine, holding that same fire of wrath in his dark eyes. "And you, Juliet, are the woman who gave me that child."

My gaping jaw snapped shut. Fuck me. "You want to have more children. With me."

His nostrils flared. "I do. And with the way you've been looking at other human babies more recently, I know you're not against having more children."

I shook my head. "What if Kenna turns out Light? What if…" *Holy mother fuck*. "What if any additional children we produce have white hair? And turn out Light, too?"

He shook his head, his jet-black hair brushing his cheeks. "Even though I truly believe that is unlikely given our birthright, I wouldn't give a shit. I want more children. Light or Dark, I don't care." Samuel's eyes narrowed on mine. "What will you do if Kenna is Dark?"

I snorted. "I'll love her just the same. I only wish for her to be Light. It's a healthier life."

"So you think." He practically rolled his eyes.

"Tell me, why haven't you returned to the Light realm with Kenna? They know about her now. What's stopping you from this 'healthier' lifestyle?"

I blinked. "You know I was talking about the energy we need to live."

"I know." He shrugged. "I thought I could find out the truth about you, though."

"My parents are assholes." I left it at that. "Back to this deal. You really can't be serious."

"I am." Again with that wicked, crooked smile. "You'll agree, too."

"Bullshit. What if I just send Kenna to the Light realm to live until her Blood Tree?"

A black brow quirked. "Do you really trust Julius to keep his hands off his mate if she's by his side constantly for another four years?"

I ground my teeth together. "Do you always have an annoying answer?"

"I like to know my prey before I go hunting." His lips twitched. "Your answer would be?"

"I don't like this."

"Neither do I."

"Then let's not do it."

A patient, humored word. My name. So much meaning behind it. "Juliet."

"Dammit!" I tossed my napkin on the table. "Fine. You have a damn deal."

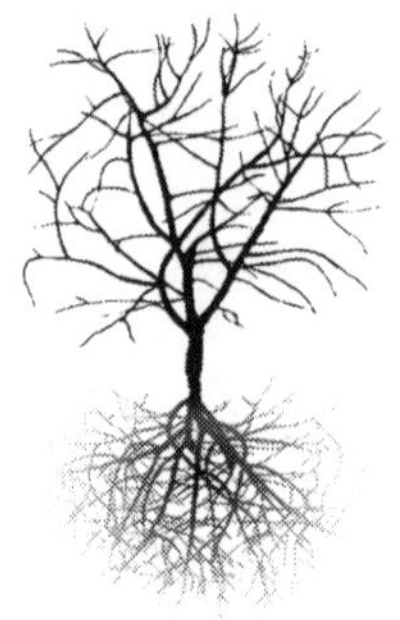

Unlocking the front door to my home, I finally spoke. "When I agreed to this, I didn't think you meant right now. I thought you meant, like on full moons when we couldn't help it." The car ride had been dead silent. Even when I ran a red light and cars honked on all sides, lost in my own nervous thoughts, we hadn't spoken. "Kenna will be home before long."

Samuel grunted. "I know. She usually gets home around eleven on a week night from the Light realm." He followed me inside, locking my door behind us. "My guards will notice if I'm gone too long so we'll make this quick."

"You could at least pretend like you don't spy on us." I blinked. "Wait. Your security team doesn't know where you are?"

He raised a black, lazy brow. "I'm reasonably sure I can take care of myself." His right hand reached for my purse, taking it off my shoulder. He tossed it across the room where it landed heavily on the recliner. "Anytime I come near you or Kenna, I leave my guards behind. No one knows about my relationship with her."

I shivered as he took a step closer. I swallowed, but my voice was a quiet breath. "That's good. I wouldn't want anyone retaliating because she's your child."

"And this is private. My personal life." He lifted both arms and ran his fingers under the edge of the spaghetti straps on my shoulders, taking another stalking step toward me and closing the distance between us. The heat from his body penetrated my trembling form, warming my frigid limbs. Despite the anger still simmering behind his thick black lashes, he was extremely gentle as he bent and wrapped his muscular arms tight around my body.

I stifled a shout as he lifted me off my feet, placing my hands on his broad shoulders. "What are you doing?"

"Taking you to your bedroom." He walked on sure feet, his destination knowing. "We can do this in there, and we'll be able to see out the back window if Kenna comes through the backyard before her usual time."

"Oh," I mumbled breathlessly. "That'll work."

He kicked my bedroom door closed behind us and glanced around my room. "You cleaned up in here." Dark eyes met mine. "I'm beginning to think your date tonight had the right idea of why you asked him out, even if you didn't consciously realize it."

I ground my teeth together. "Please pretend like you haven't been in here when my dirty clothes have been all over the place."

A head tilt to my nightstand next to my bed. "Or when you leave your vibrator out?"

My cheeks instantly flooded with color.

No words came. I was *horrified.*

Samuel winked. "I won't tell." He walked forward and promptly lowered me onto my soft mattress.

I stared wide-eyed up at him as he pulled his black sweater over his head and dropped it on my floor. My eyes drifted over all the tan and muscular flesh he had revealed. "Uh…just undress myself, huh?"

"I'm not making love to your thieving ass," he clarified carefully. His fingers were making quick work of his belt. "Hurry up and get naked. I really can't take that long tonight."

"Right," I mumbled and sat up to pull my own shirt over my head. "The quicker these…exchanges… happen, the better." Get his Dark butt out of my home. I unclipped my bra, not ashamed of my body. And neither was he from the way he was easily undressing… and hell, he seriously had nothing to worry about. His slick muscles corded in all the right places, his biceps and pecs bulging with his movements. The ribbed hills of the muscles on his stomach led down to the most perfect cock. Which was quickly hardening as he watched me undress—my struggle to wiggle out of my tight jeans a real embarrassment. I grunted as I jerked them over my hips. "But I still think you're wrong."

He sighed and leaned down, grabbing the waist of my pants, helping me. "About what?"

"Nurture versus nature."

"For an Elf, it's different. You're thinking like a

human." He threw my jeans aside and literally ripped my panties off me. "Being an Outsider can change an Elf."

As he crawled over me, my chest pumping for air, I panted, "In what way?"

His hard chest grazed my pebbled nipples and his dark eyes lifted to my wig. He raised a hand and pulled my wig off my head, my white hair spilling out onto my comforter from the careful bun I'd had it in. "It can change your way of thinking. Of the truth that an Elf and a human are not the same." His head dipped down, and his warm lips landed on my vulnerable neck. "We're not alike. Not by a long shot."

I flinched at that first touch, but his heated palms brushed my cheeks in a gentle petting, very soft for such a ruthless man, calming my nerves. His lips played at my neck, brushing and caressing until my body relaxed into the touch. My head tilted to the side, allowing him further access to my neck. His wicked lips stroked endlessly, his hands lowering to palm the swells of my breasts.

A soft moan escaped as my back arched off the bed into his touch.

He nipped my collarbone with his teeth before his moist tongue glided over the hurt. He growled a soft demand. "Quit being a coward and put your hands on me."

I groaned as I unfisted the covers I was squeezing. With hesitant actions, I lifted my arms and ran my fingers across his back. His muscles contracted under my light touch, power and man positioned over me while I was at my most vulnerable.

And he never took advantage of it.

Each brush of his hips against mine, every brush of his fingers against my most intimate flesh, the way his lips willed my body to move closer to his warmth, was all geared toward making my body susceptible for his invasion to come. I moaned as his hand landed between my thighs, his fingers sinfully talented as they played with my clit. I pressed my hands against his back and slid them down to his backside.

"Fuck, your ass is still perfect."

He chuckled quietly, lifting his head from my right breast. He flicked his tongue over my nipple, and I jerked against the touch. "I remember you saying something about it."

"Shut up." I groaned and yanked on his shoulders. "You're in a hurry. Do you remember that?"

He grunted, peering down at my mediocre sized chest. Though the way his eyes flared on them, I knew he liked what he was seeing. He bent his head and kissed each of my breasts again before lifting back over my body. "Yes, I do remember that." His knees pressed my legs apart, and he glanced once out the window before he settled his remarkable cock at the entrance to my core. "I also remember how it felt to be inside you, even if you were unskilled. You thoroughly pissed me off when you ended up Light."

My hips pressed up against his, urging him on. "So this won't be too much of a hardship?"

"Sex with a Light?" His lips twitched. "As much of a hardship as it'll be for you."

His hips slammed forward, and his cock slid deep inside me, filling me like a dream.

"Oh, fuck," I shouted. My head tipped back and my jaw dropped open.

He hissed between his teeth, "You should have thanked me for the offer. Not argued."

My fingernails dug into the muscles of his ass. "Give me more."

He grunted. "I'm letting your body adjust to my size."

"Quit with that shit and just fuck me."

His eyes narrowed. "I don't want to damage what could be my only hope—"

"My damn vagina is fine. A baby has come out of there before."

His head cocked, and his dilated eyes blinked. "Good point."

The Dark Elf's hips drove against mine, pumping his cock into me again and again. His heat and the heady scent of soap and leather surrounded me in a blanket of male dominance. He didn't allow me to speak again, his mouth landing on mine in pure ownership—it wasn't just a kiss. It was a *taking* as his tongue drove into my mouth, toying with mine and tempting me to play back.

It should have scared me, but I could only *feel* right now.

Every sensation as my nerve endings sparked to life with the demanding thrust of his hips or the way his mouth hovered over mine, baiting me to lift my head and find his lips again.

I grabbed onto his hair and yanked his head back down, smothering his soft chuckle with my mouth, our tongues colliding again. Unable to help myself, my hips lifted and met his driving plunges, our bodies smacking and slick with a sensual sweat. I shouted as he ground his pelvis against my clit, rewarding me for my enthusiasm. He rubbed back and forth against my swollen nub, and my mouth jerked from his as my head thrashed back and forth on the bed.

I hit my peak a second later, my body tingling before exploding in complete carnal heat, zapping every part of my body, and blowing my mind into wading bliss. A keening cry was my only sound as I fell over an edge so high I didn't even realize it existed. I wrapped my legs tightly around his waist and my arms around his back, not letting his body escape.

His frame tightened over mine, his fingers digging into my shoulders. He pressed his face against the side of mine as he hit his own climax. The Dark Elf convulsed against my trembling body, and his cock swelled deep inside me, pumping his seed where it needed to be.

As our bodies gradually relaxed, our limbs going slack, his words were a muffled groan against my damp hair. "That, Ladies and Gentlemen, is how you make a baby."

My giggle was breathless.

He flinched as my body vibrated. "Don't move

yet, Elf. My Dark cock is still bathing in your tight Light."

# CHAPTER 9

## *Age 40*

My shoulders hunched as I crept into my bedroom, careful of the debris littering the carpeting. I asked tentatively, "Samuel?"

*Thump.*

My chest of drawers shook at his feet where it landed, his black eyes furious with me. The muscles in his neck corded as he bellowed, "I know you're lying!"

I placed my purse on the carpet next to the red and orange watercolor painting that now had a fist-sized hole marring it, where it lay next to my feet. "Calm down." We went through this every three months. His temper was a monster only he could tame. But I always tried to help. "You know I haven't lied to you."

"Bullshit!" He stormed into my bathroom, disappearing inside. Items from my medicine cabinet started flying out the door in all directions. I ducked as my hand lotion zeroed in at my head. It smashed into a lamp farther into the room, making the thin light fixture totter back and forth. He shouted, "You have to be on some kind of contraceptive!"

I exhaled a relaxing sigh, and darted my right hand out, catching my lipstick before it crashed into the wall. "You almost hit me a second ago. You need to check yourself."

The projectile items from my bathroom instantly altered their course, aiming at the other side of the room. While his fury—and so much damn *hurt*—wasn't pleasant, he had never touched me while he was in a fit. He took care to stay far away from me while tossing items about.

"Samuel…I promise you. I haven't taken any type of birth control." My lips pinched as he stormed back into my bedroom, his chest heaving from exertion and his fingers twitching with adrenaline. My words were soft, not blaming either of us. "You know this."

His nostrils flared, and he eyed me for a full minute, scanning each of my features to discover what he feared.

The Dark Elf didn't find it, my words true.

He finally threw his palms out to his sides. "I don't understand this shit! *Four years*, Juliet. Four fucking years and not one damn missed period." He shook his head of black hair, the strands brushing his reddened cheeks. "How can that be possible?"

I peered off to the side, my attention on my closet where my clothes now scattered the floor. My voice was monotone, tragic to my own ears. "I don't know." My gut clenched as I spoke my own secret terror. "Maybe one child was all we were meant for."

"I don't believe that. I can't believe that!" He pointed a damning finger straight at me. "Your inexperienced ideas robbed me. First words. Hugs every night. A daughter's *love* and *being* there. All those special moments in Kenna's childhood are gone for me. And I'll be damned if your stubborn body deprives me of what's owed." His menacing stride ate up the distance between us.

But he placed a gentle finger against my cheek.

I sucked in a harsh breath as he pressed his hard frame against my soft curves. So much agony was hidden behind his thick lashes, only flashing through his dark eyes in a moment of weakness—like this. I spoke words I never had before, meaning them. "Samuel, I am sorry."

His black brows snapped together. "If I had done this to you, stolen your child from you, would a sorry be enough?"

I closed my eyes against the heinous act I had done, my frame trembling in shame. I fisted my hands, and my small nails dug into my flesh. "No. It wouldn't be."

His warm finger curved down my cheek, his tone choked. "I know how to please every part of your body." He removed his finger and his hand landed much lower, right on my flat stomach—not swollen with his child. "And yet your body cannot please me."

My head jerked back, his words a verbal blow. I peered up into his eyes. His stare was unforgiving and ruthless, his mouth not opening in an apology. Unbidden, tears burned my eyes. I blinked furiously to keep them at bay. I whispered again, "I'm so sorry."

Samuel held my gaze for a moment longer, glowering down at me, before he turned on his heel and marched out of my bedroom. The front door slammed, shaking my entire house.

My back slid on the wall as I fell to the ground.

The aching sobs of the barren filled my room, letting it loose with the Dark gone. The hot trickle of tears only heated my flesh further. There was no reprieve for my past actions. I had messed up. I knew that now.

And I would never have another child.

*Four years* and not even a possibility of pregnancy.

One child forever wasn't enough.

I didn't give a shit if that was selfish thinking.

I wanted another. And that man, that fucking *original* Dark Elf, had already given me the most precious and perfect offspring. I didn't want anyone else's genes mixed with mine.

I only wanted his DNA to create a baby.

Another Kenna or…God, help me, a mini-Samuel.

Strong and so full of love for others. Of hope.

I wanted *his* baby. Another precious child.

My choices had left Kenna without a father.

My actions had stolen a father's love.

But my body had failed the father this time.

All around, I was a disaster.

# CHAPTER 10

Twelve hours of sleep hadn't been enough to calm my thoughts. Samuel's words still echoed inside my head. Work was the last thing on my mind, but I pushed myself to go. Anything to erase the brutal truth of my actions would do, even if it meant staring at beauty ads and pretending I was okay to my co-workers.

I nodded to my assistant, a smile plastered on my face as I walked toward my office. I stopped at her desk and grabbed the two envelopes she handed me. "What's on my schedule for today?"

Jessica glanced at her computer screen, tapped a few buttons, and stated, "You have a meeting at one o'clock. Other than that, you're free."

"Perfect. Send a reminder to my phone about the meeting," I responded, dumping the two letters into her trashcan. Junk mail. "Buzz me if you need anything."

"Will do!" she answered with cheer.

It was about raise time. That high-pitched voice

of hers always returned once a year. The rest of the time she was halfway manageable. All I had to do was listen and her exuberant squeaking reminded me to talk to HR and give her a decent jump in salary so she would act like a normal human again—if there were such a thing.

I closed my office door behind me and placed my briefcase on my pristine glass desk. My false smile instantly fell and small wrinkles creased my forehead. I placed my hands on my lower back, and walked to the floor to ceiling windows, staring out at the Florida city. Jonas was all right to live in, not too big and not too little—everything we needed was available within a short driving distance. Kenna had adjusted well here, and she enjoyed her college studies. Having the school so close by had been a perk, allowing her to live at home still.

But she wouldn't live with me much longer.

Her Blood Tree was only two days away.

After that, she would want to live with Julius.

Her mate.

And she would leave me.

I rubbed my forehead and cleared my throat. I was going to have to find a hobby, anything to keep me busy during the transition of an empty house. I sighed out at the town and shook my hips with hardly any enthusiasm. I muttered to myself, "Maybe I'll go dancing again. I haven't done that in forever."

"I remember watching you dance once," Samuel's voice whispered from behind me somewhere. "It attracted a lot of male attention if memory serves."

I twirled around, my eyes flashing over the interior of my office. My brows puckered though in confusion, nothing out of the ordinary. An empty office except for my desk, my chair, two potted plants, my degree plaques hanging on the walls, and a guest chair facing my desk…

I paused. And really *looked.* I let my power flare.

Samuel's energy signature blazed into my line of sight. It came from across the room. He was sitting on the chair opposite my desk, facing me. Invisible to the human eye.

My lips pinched, and my voice was soft. "Have you come to say more hateful things? Or wasn't yesterday's bashing enough?"

Samuel appeared, releasing his power. He wore a pair of casual—but expensive—jeans and a gray t-shirt, his booted feet spread in a relaxed pose. But his regard was anything but calm. Beneath his hooding lashes burned a deep, quiet ache. Pain-filled black eyes stared out at me.

A crooked smile lifted his lips, void of any humor. "I've actually come to speak with you about that."

I walked forward cautiously and stopped in front of him, staring down into his eyes and crossing my arms. "What more could you have to say? I think you said it all yesterday."

His smile didn't falter. "I'm sorry."

I glanced between his eyes, holding perfectly still.

He had never apologized before.

But, then again, he had never been that unkind.

Gradually, his easy grin faltered. He sucked in a sharp breath and ran his fingers through his hair. "What I said, it was uncalled for. I never should have blamed you for us not being able to procreate again." His lips thinned into a seamless line, his tone gruff. "The entire fault may fall square on my shoulders. Not yours. As I mentioned before, I've never been able to have children. Kenna may have been an anomaly for me."

My nostrils flared as I inhaled his scent of soap and leather, the aroma soothing my nerves. "I…"

"Yes?" Samuel held my absolute attention.

I shook my head and blurted in a heady rush, "But I don't want to have children with anyone else. I don't want twenty different fathers for my children like some Elves. I only want you. Kenna *cannot* be an anomaly."

For the first time ever, Samuel was shocked. His jaw started to slack and his eyes widened enormously on his face. He even made an odd gurgling sound from the back of his throat.

I mumbled, "Surprise!"

He choked.

I tilted closer to him and pounded on his back. "Don't faint or anything too embarrassing for an original Elf. Try to breathe instead of swallowing your tongue."

He waved his hands in the air like he was swatting at a fly. "What. The. Fuck!"

My cheeks flushed to a horrible rosy hue. "This is a recent development. I haven't always felt this way."

He blinked, and then growled, "Did you feel this way when I made the deal?"

"Not exactly. But I did want more children."

"But I'm Dark. How can I be the *only* man you want to have a baby with?"

"Because you helped create Kenna."

*Our exquisite child.*

*And the Dark Elf wasn't too bad himself.*

His mouth snapped shut, and his head cocked. "Do you have a crush on me?"

I snorted. "No."

A black brow lifted. "You're lying."

I huffed. "Look, we've been having intimate sex for four years. A little bit of a crush wouldn't be unheard of."

He stared, a soft calculating pause to his person, as his black eyes ran over my features. Softly, he hummed. "And what would you say if I told you I'd been having sex with *many* Dark women during our four years together, in hopes that I could impregnate one of them?"

I took an instant step back, the air in my lungs freezing and chilling my body. I pounded on my chest, and panted, "Have you?"

*Had I really been that blind?*

*Had he been screwing other women?*

He slowly stood from his chair, watching as I sucked painfully for oxygen and gradually circling me. His eyes scanned me from head to toe before he stopped directly in front of me. A cruel black brow lifted. "You have more than a crush on me, Juliet. How could you let that happen?"

Heat flooded my face, and I bypassed his question, demanding a sharp answer for the truth. "It's not a freaking hard question to answer. Have you been having sex with other women for the past four years?"

His lips twitched, his dark eyes on mine. "No." He shrugged a shoulder. "When you're not on your period, we have sex twice a week. I didn't think it wise to ejaculate any more than that. I wanted my sperm healthy."

My cheeks puffed as I blew out a slow breath. "You always say the sweet shit."

His stared pointedly. "Now answer my question. How could you let this happen? Because if I had to guess, I'd say you're close to being in love with me." He chuckled. "And if I'd had sex with someone else, my balls would have been bruised for a week with the way your knee was twitching. You were jealous!"

"My knee did not twitch." Though I did relax my fingers from the curled fists they were in and blinked away the bull's-eye I had imagined on his face. "And there's no way in hell I'm in love with you." I paused and then chuckled a hearty laugh. "It would be ridiculous to fathom an actual loving relationship with you."

Samuel froze. "Excuse me?"

"Well, you are Dark. And an ass half the time."

His frame instantly relaxed. "But you do like me."

I shrugged a shoulder. "If you'd admit it, you like me, too."

A quiet cough, snooty words. "I think not."

My brows rose. "Did I tell you that one of my ex-lovers is moving to Jonas? He called a week ago to tell me he'd gotten a job here and—"

Dark power attacked the air in a brutal thrust of wildness, shutting down my line of conversation. He hissed viciously, "Who is this fucker? Brad the Shit Slinger or Abraham the Kiss Ass?"

I sat on the edge of my desk and swung my feet. "You know the names of the men I've slept with?" I snorted. "And Brad worked at the zoo and Abraham sold luxury cars."

"Of course, I know about them. Anyone before I landed on your doorstep, I don't know, but the two after that I watched to make sure you didn't allow them near Kenna." He waved his right hand in the air, his power still fluctuating like a flickering, faulty light-bulb. Stepping in close, he placed his hands on either side of my hips, his nose touching mine. "Now which goddamn idiot is coming to woo you back into their bed?"

It was my turn to smirk. "You're jealous."

"No, I'm just plan to kill the fucker."

"That's a *little* drastic."

Simple. Quiet. Words. "You're mine."

My lips lifted further. "Ah, but in what way?"

His mouth opened and then jammed shut.

He jerked away from me and rubbed the back of his neck. He paced one way and then the other. His dark eyes caught mine. "I don't like you like that."

I kept swinging my legs, enjoying as he squirmed in front of me. “Are you sure about that?”

“I…”

I quirked a white brow. “Yes?”

He pivoted and walked straight to my door. “I have a meeting I need to take care of. We’ll talk about this silliness later.”

I waved at his retreating backside. “I’m sure we will.”

Samuel threw open the door but stopped cold.

His body was still visible. He had forgotten.

Jessica’s head snapped up from her computer, her shock at seeing him inside my office flashing away. She beamed, her smile so bright. My assistant asked quickly, “Is there something I can help you with?”

Samuel stared at her, and then rubbed at his left ear. He glanced back at me, and muttered, “I would never put up with that shit. She sounds like she has an addiction to carnival balloons. You should fire her ass.”

With that, he charged down the hallway toward the elevators, quickly rounding a corner, no longer in sight.

I shoved off my desk and patted the air. “It’s all right, Jessica. He comes off that way to everyone.”

She blinked. “Like an asshole?”

“Yes.” I shut the door and turned to my desk.

Samuel was right on one account—I had work to do. I dug my cell phone out of my briefcase and dialed. Placing my phone to my ear, I sighed in relief when she answered. “Susan, I have a project that requires your assistance. Is there any way you could steal some literature from the library there? I'm going to the cabin tonight and could use some reading material to pass out to. I want everything you can find on the original Elves."

# CHAPTER 11

I closed the remaining book Susan had brought me last night and tucked it under my bed for safe keeping. The ache in my eyes reminded me I had been reading for quite a while. I rubbed at them while glancing at my alarm clock on my nightstand.

My brows lowered. Kenna was late for our movie marathon—not completely uncommon for her. But she was a good two hours late. I leaned to the side and grabbed my cell phone lying on the far pillow.

I dialed her number.

Kenna didn't answer.

"Excuse me, daughter," I mumbled with irritated flare. Kids never changed no matter how old they were. I dialed her again. Listened to the ringing, and then her voicemail. My lips thinned, but I waited for the beep. "Kenna, it's Mom. Where are you? Call me back before I get worried."

I glanced at the clock again and rubbed my right brow. Tomorrow was her Blood Tree. She wouldn't be running around and skipping our night together over nothing. I nibbled on my bottom lip and tried her number again after ten minutes of no return phone call.

My daughter didn't pick up.

I gradually stood from my bed and paced the bedroom floor. I watched the clock tick by, minute after minute. And yet my phone never rang.

She'd said she was going to the diner before picking up the cloak from the cleaners. There was a chance that Samuel had been there. That was his destination of choice for getting to know her better, keeping it private and easygoing.

I only hesitated a moment before calling him. I never phoned him directly. He had given me his number in case of emergencies—and *only* for emergencies since his men were constantly around him. All other times, he called me.

He answered on the second ring, and promptly ordered, "Give me a second." There were multiple rowdy voices in the background, so I kept quiet. A minute later, with much less noise buzzing on his end, he asked quietly, "What's wrong?"

"Were you with Kenna today? She said she was going to the diner."

"Yes, I was there. We talked for a while."

"Well, she's not home for movie night yet. And she's not answering her phone." I sighed. "I'm worried now. I don't think she'd miss our last night like this on purpose."

He was quiet for a long second and then cursed

quietly. “I knew something was wrong when she left. She was in a rush to get somewhere.”

“The laundry mat. She was picking up the cloak she’s going to wear tomorrow. It’s the one I wore at my Blood Tree.” One of the possessions I had made sure to take the night I left my parents. “Is there any way you could swing by—”

His voice was winded. “I’m already on my way out of the Dark realm. What’s the address?”

I rattled it off to him. “Call me when you get there. I’ll keep trying her cell phone.”

“Of course.” He hung up.

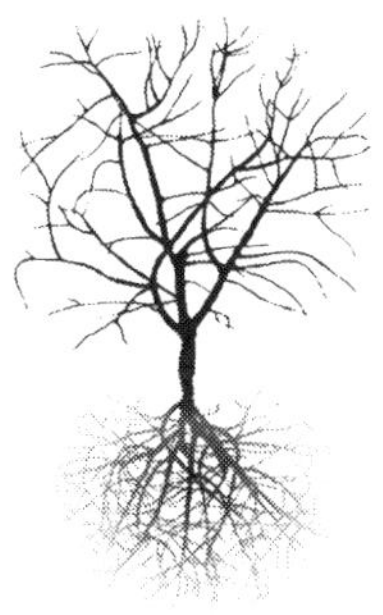

My phone vibrated in my hand two hours later. I quickly answered, growling with anxiety, “Did you find her? She’s still not here.”

“She was at the cleaners,” he stated in a soothing tone. “There was a small mess she left behind, but I’ve cleaned that up. And I’ve located her and she’s fine.”

“Tell me where.”

He hummed softly. “I’m reasonably sure she

wants to be alone tonight. She's safe, so don't worry. I'll watch over her."

The wrinkles in my forehead never cleared. "What do you mean she wants to be alone?" I paused. "And what did you mean by she left a mess at the cleaners?" My eyes widened, his words of her being in a rush to leave the diner hitting home. "She didn't break in there or anything, did she?"

Samuel snorted. "The cloak is in the backseat of her car."

I sighed in exasperation, my shoulders lowering in supreme relief. "I still think I should be with her if she's feeling guilty."

"No…" He paused and then snorted. "Oh, my. Our darling daughter just stole a bottle of booze from a homeless man. I really don't think she wants company right now."

I stared blindly at my bedroom wall. "Buy that man another bottle."

"I'll buy him a few. He appears very put out."

"I can imagine." I rubbed at my forehead. "Well, I'll keep trying her phone anyway. Maybe she'll answer if she wants to come home tonight."

Another soft hum. "She probably won't."

"You'll stay to protect her?"

"Always."

"Okay, I'll see you at the Blood Tree tomorrow then." I tapped on my bottom lip with a pointed finger. "And tomorrow night, I think we should talk."

"Agreed. We didn't finish our conversation yesterday."

*Because you ran away*. "Perfect."

He was silent a long moment. "Juliet?"

"Hmm?"

"Have you prepared yourself if she's Dark?"

"She'll be Light. I know it."

He coughed, and then laughed. "It's always best to be prepared for any situation. Especially when you're in front of the entire Elf race."

My face scrunched. "I suppose my parents *will* be there. Maybe you're right." Though I highly doubted they would even look at me let alone speak to me. Bastards. "I'll think about it."

"Just keep your chin up. After all, you're in love with one Dark Elf. What's loving another one really going to do?"

"Good God. I do *not* love you."

He snorted. "So you say."

"So I know."

Samuel snickered. "Good night, Juliet."

"Keep our girl safe, Samuel."

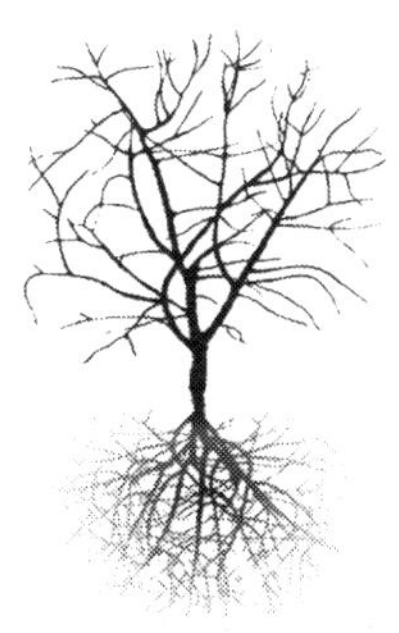

I charged through the front door of my house. My attention honed on the Dark Elf sitting on my couch. I glared so furiously his head would have a hole in it if my eyes were bullets.

Samuel raised is hands…though an enormous crooked grin gradually lifted his lips. "Don't be mad at me. I told you nature always won over nurture with an Elf."

The muscles ticked in my cheeks as I ground my teeth together. I whispered, "Where is she?"

"She just got in the shower, I think."

Okay then. I raised my voice. "Why the fuck didn't you tell me the 'mess' you cleaned up last night was a dead motherfucking body?"

He shrugged. "I knew you would freak out."

I shook my hands in the air, my eyes wide. "Hell yes, I would have! My daughter had just been attacked and *killed* a man!" More hand shaking. "A mother has a right to freak out over that. Instead, you left me to look like a fool during her Blood Tree in front of the entire Elf nation!"

"Actually, I did warn you—"

"Shut up!" I panted.

Again, my eyes were shooting bullets.

Samuel cleared his throat, and stated softly, "You didn't appear a fool either. Only shocked. And you recovered nicely, too." He scratched his chin. "I remember this one time, where this parent—"

"I don't give a fuck," I muttered and let my back fall against the wall. All the fight in me drained from my system, and my head fell into my palms. My voice was muffled by my hands as I whispered, "My daughter is Dark."

Samuel hummed. "As I thought she would be."

I peeked up at him and rolled my eyes. "You don't have to be so damn arrogant about it."

He relaxed back on the couch and placed his hands behind his head, pulling his t-shirt tight against his muscular pecs and biceps. He didn't miss how his body affected me either, a small cocky chuckle vibrating deep in his chest. "It's not Tuesday yet. You still have three more days until our next encounter." A black brow lifted. "Unless you'd like to have a quickie tonight when I come back from my training session with Kenna."

I blinked. "We aren't going to finish our previous conversation like we planned?"

"Not right now. I can tell she needs energy. The more powerful the Elf after their Blood Tree, the faster they need it to energize their body."

"Oh." I dropped my hands to my sides, realizing how ridiculous I appeared with them half hiding my face. "That'll work, I guess."

His lips twitched. And he flexed his biceps. "To the quickie? Or to the talk?"

I sent my eyes skyward. "Lord, help me."

"I'll take that as both."

*Bang. Bang. Bang.*

I jerked up straight from the wall and turned my attention to my front door. The person had knocked so hard the wood might be dented on the other side. My brows puckered, and I took a step toward the door.

But I quickly hopped back when the front door burst open…and a furious original Light Elf stormed inside. My white brows lifted, plenty irked at the man. He had been an asshole to my daughter tonight. I stepped into his path, barring his way to the hallway. "Julius."

His dark eyes flicked once to Samuel, sneered, and then snapped back to mine. "Get out of my way. I want to know exactly what the hell happened last night."

"Hmm." My nose crinkled, and I shook my head. "I don't think so. Not in the mood you're in right now." I flicked my right hand toward the door. "Go cool off, and then you can come back later and *apologize* for how you behaved."

He jammed a pointed finger over my shoulder, barking, "That is my mate in there. I have every right —"

"She is *my* daughter, and you are in *my* house. We're not in the Light realm right now. You will do as I say."

His hands landed on my shoulders, his black eyes filled with pure possession. "My mate. And you will do as I say or I will—"

"Get your fucking hands off her, Julius," Samuel growled so quietly, his tenor filled with so much terror, the original Light Elf and I froze. Our heads tilted to the side. Samuel now stood only an inch away from us, his power vibrating on the air, stabbing in Julius's direction. "Or *I* will make you move."

Julius's white brows furrowed, but he jerked his

hands back and stared at his palms. We stood in tension-filled silence until Julius dropped his hands and peered up at me. "I'm sorry. I will leave and come back later when I'm no longer in shock."

I crossed my arms. Nodded. "And you'll apologize to your mate."

He rubbed at his chest, his words hesitant. "I didn't handle her Blood Tree well, did I?"

I snapped, "Not in the least."

Julius swallowed heavily. "I just can't believe it."

"Believe it," Samuel muttered. "She's Dark."

Julius cast a withering glance in his direction.

I gestured to my still open door. "Go on."

He growled under his breath.

But he turned and walked out of my house.

Samuel slammed the door behind him, almost hitting him in the backside. "Fucking Light prick."

A squeak came from Kenna's bedroom, her shower shutting off. I moved toward the couch and sat. "She'll be out soon." I rubbed at my forehead. "And I can take care of Julius. I don't need your help with him."

Samuel snorted and dropped onto the love seat. "If you think for one second you could handle Julius in a fight, you seriously need to check your ego."

"He wouldn't fight me."

"For his mate?" Black, incredulous brows lifted. "He would make you disappear in a heartbeat if you actually came between the two of them together. That Elf has been waiting for his mate forever."

My eyes narrowed. "I can protect my child."

"Not against him," Samuel hissed, keeping his tone down. Kenna was banging around in her room, finishing getting ready. He shook his dark head of hair. "And I do not want him touching you."

I arched a brow. Smirked. "Why is that?"

He scowled. "We'll talk about this later *like I said.*"

I clicked my teeth a few times, eyeing him. "You're more than a little bit ridiculous. Even for a Dark Elf."

"And you're more than a little bit close-minded. Even for a Light Elf."

Kenna's door clicked shut.

We both glanced away from each other. Mute.

She stopped dead in her tracks inside the living room. "You two will learn to get along with each other."

I snorted.

Samuel grunted.

She persisted, not understanding. "The Light and the Dark aren't that different."

Our heads swung to her, our eyes on our daughter.

*Had she heard us talking?*

She clarified, "They both feed off humans."

*Thank God.* She hadn't heard us.

We glanced away.

I snorted.

Samuel grunted.

Kenna murmured, "Well, this is fun."

I snorted at the same time Samuel grunted.

"Okay, that was enough time spent together for

the first evening." Kenna waved a hand at Samuel. "Let's go feed on some drug dealers."

My attention snapped to Samuel. Being Light would have been so much healthier for our daughter. I brought back my bullet eyes and glared with all my might. It was going to take some getting used to—my daughter being Dark. And all that it brought along with it.

# CHAPTER 12

Sitting out back, I sipped on my third—or fourth—double shot of vodka. Julius had finally left and Kenna had eventually gone to bed. I was now waiting for a Dark Elf to come through my back gate. When he arrived twenty minutes later, I gestured to the patio chair next to me. "Take a seat. We need to have this conversation in a hurry."

Samuel's black brows furrowed as he took a seat, stretching his legs out in front of him. "Why the rush?"

"I'll explain after our talk." I downed the rest of my liquor and sat the empty glass on the table between us. With the time restraint on us, I peered directly into his eyes. My words were honest and blunt—thank you liquid courage. "I do want to be in a romantic relationship with you. I understand that now."

He stared back, his lashes hooding his eyes. "So I was right. You are in love with me."

I shook my head. "No, not yet. But I do like you." I cleared my throat. "Possibly a lot."

Samuel tapped his fingers on the table. "How would you propose a romantic relationship could even exist?"

"Well, our daughter and Julius are going to make it work. I see no reason why we couldn't go on dates, too."

He eyed me. "That would not work. I am the original Dark Elf. My people are not as *friendly* as the Light Elves."

"You'd worry about my safety?"

"That's an understatement."

My lips pinched into a thin line. "They'll know about Kenna, eventually. Therefore, me in the process."

"True. But what happened between us would be in the past in their eyes. You wouldn't be a target for them."

I mumbled, "I don't really want our daughter to be a target either."

"They won't mess with her. Julius being her mate is enough to scare them off. A mate is not something anyone would mess with." His fingers kept tapping, his lips twitching. "So what else would you suggest?"

My nose crinkled. "We could keep it private."

His dark gaze ran over my features. "You're not fond of that idea."

"Not particularly."

He hummed. "Keep thinking."

My attention shot toward him and his teasing tone. I focused past the alcohol in my system. Humor danced deep in his eyes, directed straight at me. I questioned, "What aren't you saying?"

"I think I already said it."

I rubbed my forehead. "Just tell me. I've had a few too many vodkas."

"You're cute when you're tipsy." He snickered and leaned forward, resting his arms on the table. "If you're serious about this, we could always say we're mated."

My jaw dropped. "Uh…"

His crooked grin curved his lush lips. "Yes?"

I stuttered, "I said I wanted to try a romantic relationship with you. If we said I was your mate, then we would be together forever."

"Or until I found my actual mate."

I instantly glared. "Have you been playing your flute?"

He snickered softly and tilted to the side. He pulled something out of his back pocket and held it between us. "I brought it with me." He set it down on the table and scooted it toward me. "And I'm giving it to you."

I grabbed the damn thing and held it close to my chest, not even caring that it showed just how much I didn't want him to find his real mate. "I'll keep it." I peered down my nose at him. "For now."

His lips twitched. "I thought you might."

My head cocked as I scanned his tan features. "So I was right. You do like me."

He shrugged one shoulder and leaned back on

his chair. "It took some self-evaluation on my part." He winked. "But, yes. I do like you. Possibly a lot."

I tapped my bottom lip with the tip of his flute, watching him. "You're serious about the mate business."

He nodded. "I am."

"You really think this could work for us then. Like, *forever* work."

"All relationships have their bumps and bruises. It won't always be rainbows. But if I'm going to spend my time with any woman, I would prefer it be you."

I lifted the flute and stared at it, wishful thinking overwhelming me. "You don't think that—"

"You said you were in a hurry. If I play that right now, and you are my mate, then we'll pass out for some time." He shrugged and reached for the flute. "I'll play it right now if you want—"

I yanked the flute back from his hand. "Nope, not right now. No time for that." I glanced at my watch. "We need to have sex."

Samuel blinked. "Explain."

"I have a theory about the original Elves I want to test." I stood from my chair and waved at him to hurry and stand. "Seriously, I'll explain it as we walk to my bedroom." I cast a warning glance at him. "We have to be quiet, though. Kenna's home and sleeping."

"All right." He followed me inside.

As I walked, I whispered over my shoulder, "The original Light and Dark Elves were created from the Garden of Eden after Eve disobeyed God. One Light. One Dark."

"Yes, I remember."

We snuck into my bedroom, and I quickly shut the door behind us—locked it. I yanked my shirt over my head and tossed it aside, watching as his strong fingers started undoing his belt. "The Blood Tree *spoke* to you and Julius. You were each given the right to create ten new beings by sacrificing your own blood onto the tree."

"Yes." He kicked his shoes off before removing his pants. His shirt hit the floor next. "Your point?"

"The *Blood Tree* is my point." I stared with wonder, my idea actually taking root. "We got pregnant the night of my own Blood Tree. Since you're an original Elf, I think you can only create new beings when a blood sacrifice has been made to the tree, as you did in the beginning. The night the Blood Tree receives its due." I pointed at the clock, showing there were only fifteen minutes left to this night. "And if I'm right, we need to get to it."

Samuel didn't blink, his eyes on mine. Thoughts ran amok inside that ancient head of his, scouring my theory for any holes. And from the way he ripped his boxers off, I knew he had found none.

He yanked on my feet, pulling me flat onto the bed. "We're going to make a baby."

"We're sure as hell going to try."

# CHAPTER 13

I stared out through the curtains of my house the next day.

My daughter had left Julius and Samuel outside.

Alone.

Kenna hadn't needed to order me to watch them. My eye was on my man. We were going to tell Kenna the news in a few minutes—who her father really was. Julius would be in on the revealing, too. He would need to be one of the first to know in order to prepare for any backlash and protect his mate.

But Kenna rushed back out into the living room.

She had a night bag full of items over her shoulder.

I dropped the edge of the curtain and straightened. "Where do you think you're going?"

"Julius said he has a surprise for me. He's taking me out tonight." Kenna's lips twitched. "All night if I have my way."

And I was sure her mate wouldn't mind that. I

cleared my throat and crossed my arms, peering down the end of my nose at her. "I wanted to speak with you and Julius tonight."

Her shoulders instantly sagged, her green eyes caught on mine. My daughter whined so prettily. "Does it have to happen tonight? He seemed really excited, and with that look on your face, I don't want to ruin our evening."

I inhaled heavily, evaluating her situation. I came to a decision when she started bouncing on the balls of her feet and edging toward the front door. "Fine. But we really do need to talk tomorrow. I want you both here at a decent time."

She nodded with enthusiasm. "I promise."

I rolled my eyes as she ran out the door. I followed her motion and stopped to hold the door open. Kenna jumped on Julius's back, wrapping her arms around his neck and her legs around his waist. He caught her easily, holding her in place by her thighs even as he finished his conversation with Samuel.

Julius carried Kenna down the driveway, tilting his head to the side and kissing her cheek.

Samuel peered at me with a question in his eyes.

I groaned and shook my head. "Tomorrow."

He waited until they were out of sight before he strolled up to my front porch. He leaned against the doorframe, a small smile flirting on his lips. "So…how long do we have?"

I waggled my brows at him and grabbed the front of his shirt, yanking him inside. I kicked the door shut and locked it absently, my eyes on his. "They'll be gone all night."

"I thought so." Samuel gripped my wig and dropped it to the floor, and ran his fingers through my long hair that spilled out. "He was telling me he bought a resort. For them to live at. He's going to show her right now."

I blinked, holding still. "He's taking her away?"

"You knew it would happen."

I released a shuddering breath. "It doesn't make it any easier." I cracked my neck from side to side. "How far away is it?"

"Not far. Well within driving distance." His lips curved up. "And the resort will be open for Dark and Light Elves."

My eyes widened comically. "How big is the place?"

"Julius was very proud of it, so I would say it's big enough to add two more people without stepping on any toes."

My hips did a little shimmy. "Hell yes."

He tugged on a lock of my hair. "How about I play you a song before our evening really begins?"

I sucked in a harsh breath. "Are you sure you want to test it?"

"No better time than the present." He chuckled softly. "And if you're not my mate, you can burn the flute like you were talking about in your sleep last night."

I choked. "I don't talk in my sleep!"

"You do." He pinched his fingers together. "A little."

I glared but moved away from him to retrieve the flute…where it was hidden in the fireplace. My glare was enough that he didn't say a word when I handed it back to him, soot covered and all.

Though he did laugh full and loud. "We're going to be one hell of an interesting couple."

"I would concur." I pointed at the flute. "Now play me a damn song so I know to buy more firewood or not."

He grinned and pressed it to his lips, his dark eyes never leaving mine. "Truth time."

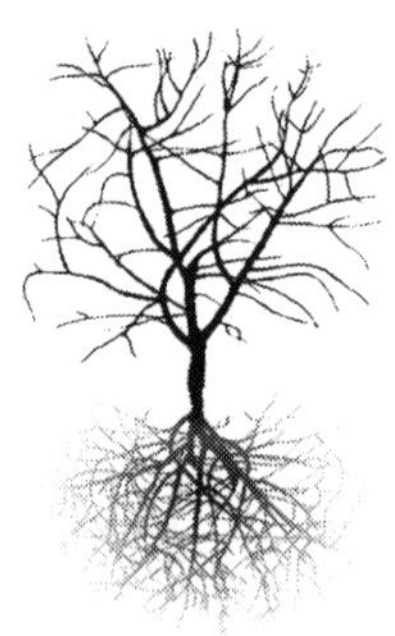

*"Oh my God!"* Kenna shrieked.

My head whipped off my pillow. "Huh?"

A male cough was followed by Julius rumbling swiftly, "Excuse us. We'll…be waiting in the living room." Another cough, choking down a laugh. "For that news you wanted to tell us."

"Get her the hell out of here, Julius," Samuel rumbled next to me. "Dammit!"

I rubbed the sleep out of my eyes and squinted through the afternoon light. My daughter stood stalk still right inside my bedroom door, her mouth hanging open, as Julius gently placed his hand on her back and prodded her out of my room.

Kenna muttered from the hallway, sounding shocked as hell, "She said she wanted us here at a decent time."

Julius's voice was garbled. "By the look of things, I don't think she meant this early."

"But...but...that was *Samuel*."

"I believe I noticed that."

"I don't understand." A pause. "They don't even *like* each other." Quick, questioning words. "Maybe they got drunk?"

"Kenna, let's just wait for them to come out here."

"Okay, okay. Yes. That's right." Her head peeked back into my bedroom. She pointed to the right. "We'll just be in the living room."

My words were dry by this point. "Yes, we heard." I held the blanket close to my naked chest. "Samuel and I will be out there shortly."

Samuel groaned when their footsteps headed away from my bedroom. He dropped back onto my mattress. "That was not the way I wanted to tell her about us."

I patted his hand. "Well, we still get to control the situation when we tell her you're her father."

"*Oh my fucking God!*" Kenna shouted from the hallway. "Did she just say he's my *dad?*"

Samuel's eyes narrowed on me. "Smooth."

I grimaced. "We need to hurry and fix this."

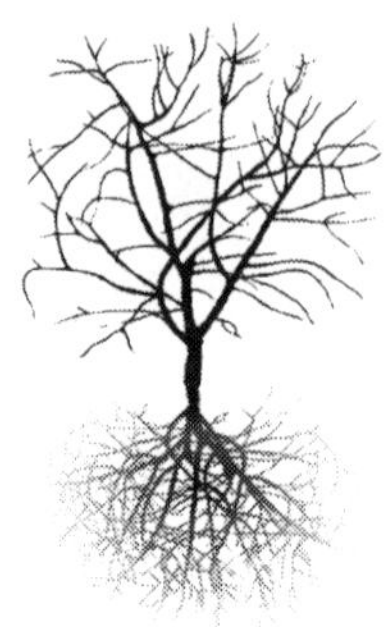

Kenna sat on the couch, her mate's arm wrapped tightly around her shoulder and holding her close. Those bullet-eyes she had were definitely inherited from me, and she was using them to her full advantage as she glared across the living room where Samuel and I stood side-by-side.

She finally growled, "This is bullshit."

I cleared my throat. "I'm sorry for not telling you sooner. It's long and complicated, but I wanted you to have a real shot at being Light." A finger flick at Samuel. "Even with having an original for a father."

Our daughter scratched at her right arm and skewered Samuel with her scrutiny. "How long have you known I'm your kid?"

His tone was patient. "Since you were thirteen. I eventually tracked you guys down every time you moved and evaluated the situation. I don't make decisions lightly, and your whole life had already begun —without me in it. It was my choice to wait until your Blood Tree to tell you."

Green eyes flicked to me. She didn't speak for a full five minutes. My legs began to cramp before she opened her mouth. "You were that worried I would be Dark?"

I nodded. "At first."

"And then?"

"Later, I came to realize I didn't care. But Samuel was right. Your life had too much craziness in it at the time to add a newfound parent to the mix." I swallowed on a dry throat. My eyes never altered from my daughter, from the actions I had done. "Given what I know now, I would do things much differently, but at the time, I was young. I had grown up in the Light realm my entire life, and I only knew the Dark were Elves to despise. I'm not giving excuses, but it's the truth."

Julius tilted his head, his dark eyes on Samuel. "How long have you two been together?"

"A while," Samuel stated elusively. He shook his head, his eyes turning back to our daughter. "I am sorry too if my choices have hurt you."

Her dark brows puckered. "That's the thing. I'm not hurt. Not exactly. I'm mad that I've been lied to for so long." Her regard danced between us. "I can understand why each of you did what you did. But it still stings that you weren't honest."

"I'm so sorry," Samuel and I said in unison.

It was quiet for another five minutes.

Them staring at us. Us staring back.

Finally, Kenna grumbled, "This is one fucked-up situation."

Nods occurred all around.

Samuel wrapped his around my waist and pulled me close to him. "And the news isn't done yet."

Julius's brows lifted, and then he swiftly peered down to his mate. "Do you need a break first?"

"No." She rubbed his right leg. "Might as well get it done in one shot."

That's my girl.

I grinned and ran my own arms around Samuel's waist, hugging him in return. "Well, Kenna, this isn't bad news."

Samuel chuckled quietly and kissed my forehead. He peered back to our daughter. "Your mother is my mate."

Julius froze.

Kenna blinked. "Really."

*Yes. Really.*

*His song had called to me.*

I cleared my throat. "Yes. We were unconscious for about half the night before we woke up. That's why we slept so late today."

"You just found out?"

"Yes."

Kenna stared…and then a full grin lifted her features. "Congratulations. I was worried about you being alone when I left."

Samuel raised a finger. "About that." His

attention swung to Julius, his tone innocent. "Do you have room for two more at the Haven Resort?"

Julius stared. "Oh. Fuck me."

Samuel winked. "Nah. I've got your mate's mom for that." My mate ran his hand over my lower stomach, rubbing softly. "I'm sure you can make do with us there, right?"

Kenna instantly stated, "Of course!"

Julius glared behind her head.

And Samuel grinned. "Good. I want to know you even more than I already do. I want to become the father you should have had."

Kenna didn't flinch at his pronouncement, her tone somewhat shy. "I would like that."

Julius's narrowed eyes were stuck on Samuel's petting hand, his own words soft. "Dammit. Is she pregnant, too?"

Samuel chuckled. "We hope so." A gentle shake of his head, even while he smiled. "We'll see. Time will tell."

I peered up into my mate's eyes. "Even if we're not, we have each other."

"Forever." He kissed my lips softly. "Always."

# SUSAN'S STORY

# CHAPTER 1

## *Age 232*

Randor was ticking me off.

If he wanted to know something, that was what a stinking phone was for. But no. He wanted me to talk to Julius in person. And since Julius was at Juliet's house this afternoon, apparently, I was the logical pick—since Randor couldn't leave his newfound duties in the Light realm for all of fifteen minutes.

Prick.

Taking over for Julius was going to make his freaking ego that much bigger.

I grumbled under my breath and stopped at Juliet's backdoor. I didn't bother to knock. I merely walked in. My friend had finally forgiven me, Kenna's Blood Tree completed, and my favor owed was paid in full. Not that friending Kenna had been a hardship. I really did like the young girl—even if she'd had 'Dark' written all over her actions from the day I met her.

I paused inside the back door as I heard voices filtering from the living room. My white brows rose at one of the men I could hear. It was Samuel, the original Dark Elf. The others conversing were the voices of Juliet, Julius, and Kenna. With quiet movements, I closed—and locked—the backdoor.

I eavesdropped. No shame here either.

Gradually, my right hand rose to cover my mouth.

Juliet and Samuel were mates. *Holy crap!*

Julius growled, "Dammit. Is she pregnant, too?"

My eyes widened in shock, holding very still for the response.

Samuel's chuckle was pure victory. "We hope so." He paused a moment, amending himself. Hopeful words. "We'll see. Time will tell."

"Even if we're not, we have each other," Juliet stated softly—dang tender actually.

"Forever," Samuel crooned. "Always."

I choked back my shock, shaking my head past all the lovey-dovey crap.

It was time I made my appearance. Randor had said he needed a response fast.

I ran my fingers through my white hair, fixing the strays that had blown in the breeze from my jog here. I had one foot forward when I heard my ruler clear his throat. Loudly.

Julius barked, "Susan, quit being nosey and get your ass in here now."

Samuel snickered quietly. "I wondered how long you were going to give her."

I instantly scowled. It was hard spying on Elves as powerful as them, my power signature giving me away…every dang time. I thrust my shoulders back, and muttered, "Coming."

Julius muttered, "Shut up, asswipe. I wasn't talking to you."

Samuel was very pleased with himself, if his tone was any indication. "Now, Julius, is that any way to treat an old friend who will be living under your roof soon?"

"Old, yes. Friend, fuck no." He grunted. "I didn't say you could live there anyway."

"Ah…but you do owe me a favor."

Julius was quiet, and then started cursing up a storm.

I kept from laughing as I turned into the living room. Somehow, the Dark Elf had wrangled a favor out of my ruler—and he wasn't pleased with it at all. I didn't falter when his sharp gaze flayed me, his anger wasn't for me. "Sir, if I may interrupt," a little late for that, "Randor has a question he would like answered."

White brows puckered. "And he sent you?" A blink. "Instead of calling?"

"Yes." I sighed heavily, my chest rising and lowering with my exasperation. "I don't understand either, but when the stand-in ruler calls…I must obey." I would rather be buried alive for a hundred years than say that again, but I would do my duty to the Light realm.

Julius dipped his head, his arms never leaving their captive embrace of his mate—who was decidedly fragile in appearance giving the news she had just received. "Tell me."

I tried not to roll my eyes. I couldn't believe I was here saying this. It had to be some type of joke on Randor's part. "The message is as such: White bread is better than wheat bread."

Now, given the ridiculous nature of what had just come out of my mouth, I didn't expect the response that came forth. In fact, I took two quick steps backward when Julius was instantly in front of me, his dark eyes like razors. He grabbed my right bicep, glanced over his shoulder at the other occupants of the room, stating, "We'll be back in a moment."

Samuel whistled quietly, holding his mate in his arms easily. "Trouble?"

"Fuck. Off." Julius started marching straight to the back of the house, pulling me along with him. My feet pattered to keep up with his larger strides, my shock worn off. Randor's message had been code, my direct mission to bring our ruler the news not so stupid. I kept quiet until Julius stopped hauling my ass out of the house, both of us standing on the sunlit back lawn, the screen door banging closed behind us. Julius released my arms and stared straight up into the sky, his white brows drawn together, deep in thought. "Did he say anything else?"

"Yes." My lips pinched. "Butter is better than jam."

Julius growled and rubbed his hands over his face. "So it's not immediate then." More rubbing of his face, then he tilted his attention back to me. His eyes held mine, but I knew his mind was still working in his silence. My ruler didn't even blink. Dark eyes so full of knowledge eventually closed. They stayed that way as he shook his head. "I can't do it. Not with the information I've just learned."

The heat of the sun beat down on us, a bead of sweat trickling down my spine. "Is there a message you want me to return?"

His eyes flashed open. "Yes."

I waited.

He still didn't seem convinced with his choice, his jaw muscles clenching. "Tell Randor…"

Another bead of sweat dripped down my right temple.

He sighed and nodded his head once. "Tell him no action is needed."

# CHAPTER 2

Incredible blue eyes stared as if I had lied. "Tell me *exactly* what he said."

I crossed my arms, my nostrils flaring. "I did."

A direct order. "Say it again."

"He said no action is needed." My teeth ground together. "Look, Randor, I don't know what the heck is going on, but I'm telling the truth."

He jerked to stand from his chair. Julius's chair, inside Julius's office. This man was taking his new position seriously. Though he hadn't messed with the pencils that Julius was so anal about, leaving those alone in the mug where they were held—in the tacky Santa-Ninja cup that Kenna had bought him one Christmas. No one messed with 'The Mug.'

Randor's muscles rippled under his white shirt as he prowled to stand directly in front of me. I barely breathed, not wanting to scent him, the cologne he favored. Because he smelled so dang good. I had to keep this business or I would clam up and become the mute idiot I hated so much when he was nearby. His head cocked, his sparkling blue eyes running over my features ever so slowly. An eyebrow lifted. "What else aren't you telling me?"

My teeth would be down to nubs by the time I left here if I kept clenching my jaw as I was. "I don't know what you're talking about."

"Julius would never have ordered a 'stand down' if something else hadn't happened."

I blinked. "Well, I did overhear some interesting information while I was there."

The other eyebrow lifted. "You were eavesdropping again?"

My eyes narrowed. "Do you want to hear it or not?"

He rested his hips back against the desk, careful not to disturb 'The Mug.' He flicked a hand, all cocky and in command. "I'm waiting."

"Samuel was at Juliet's house, too."

His gaze was unflinching. "And? Kenna is his subject now."

I shook my head and leaned forward, speaking quietly just in case anyone was close by outside the office. "I think he spent the night there." I pointed at my head. "His hair was a mess and he looked pretty dang comfortable."

Randor's adorable forehead crinkled. "No way."

I nodded. "It gets better." My lips curved in amusement, knowing the news would blow him away if he didn't believe the Dark Elf would have sex with a Light Elf. "Juliet is his mate."

Stunned. He sat there stunned, his jaw gaping open. An odd gurgling noise escaped past his throat. The look suited him, making him more 'real.'

I rolled a finger. "Want to know something else?"

He nodded his head…if you counted another gurgling noise as a nod.

"Samuel is Kenna's father."

His eyes flew wide open, and he shouted, "Holy shit!"

My nose crinkled. "You really don't need to cuss. But, yes, I agree."

He straightened and started pacing the room between me and the desk, traveling back and forth at a slow pace. His fingers massaged his forehead as he stared at the carpeting beneath his feet. Randor's next words were hesitant, almost like he didn't want to ask. "Is there anything else?"

I shrugged my right shoulder. "I think Samuel and Juliet are trying to have another baby. Samuel said it's possible that she could be pregnant again."

"Holy motherfucking Blood Tree." Randor jerked to a halt an inch away, and shook his head. "No wonder he wants me to stand down."

Curiosity got the better of me. I tilted in his direction, asking softly, "Stand down from what?"

Randor snorted. He wasn't so shocked that he would give me private information.

Dang handsome, intelligent, manipulative man.

He shook his head, his gaze steadfast on my brown eyes. With the patience of a predator, he lifted his left hand and tucked one of my stray white locks behind my ear. I held perfectly still at the touched, his fingers warm and rough against my soft flesh. All my thoughts disappeared except for this gentle moment, my mouth turning dry and my words gone.

Randor watched my expression as he always did when his body came into contact with mine. His other hand raised, and he tucked another curl behind my other ear. Wide red lips on a ruggedly sexy face tilted up, his words soft. "I need you to do something for me."

My mouth bobbed. Not a sound escaped.

His eyes crinkled at the corners, and he bent to place his face in front of mine. "I need you to watch Kenna's actions for the next couple of days. Don't let them know you're there so stay far back from Julius." His thumb brushed my cheek. "Can you handle that?"

"Mmm." That was a yes.

Heady, he smelled so scrumptious. I just wanted to lean in a little more.

He caught my shoulder when I did, my action almost causing me to tumble on my face.

But…his arm wrapped around me, holding me steady.

I didn't even mind the blush staining my cheeks.

"Careful," he whispered. His heated breath fanned my lips, and mine parted on their own accord, ready to accept his kiss if he would just lower his head a wee bit more. Those delectable lips grinned, flashing his blinding white smile down on me. "Susan?"

"Mmm."

"I have another meeting planned now. They're knocking on the door."

I blinked furiously and quickly shoved away from him. My gaze shot to the door where, indeed, someone was knocking. "Sorry." I messed with my hair, stumbling toward the door. Butterflies had taken up residence in the pit of my stomach, and my hands were trembling. "I'll get right on that job."

Calm words. "Thank you." A beat. "Call me immediately if you notice anything out of the norm. Do not engage. Understand?"

"Yeah," I mumbled. I opened the door quickly and maneuvered around Kent. Randor was meeting with the second in command of security. I nodded respectfully to him. "Kent."

Kent eyed my flushed cheeks. His lips twitched. "Hello, Susan. It looks like Randor was his usual charming self."

I stared, my blush flaring even worse.

"Get your ass in here," Randor griped. He grabbed a fistful of Kent's shirt and yanked him into the office. Blue eyes stared down at me, his words soft. "Remember, Susan. Do not engage. Call me first."

I flicked a finger in a quick salute. "Of course." I wasn't in the first hundred years of my life, after all. I did have a few years experience under my belt. "I'll call you."

He hummed softly, his gaze running over my features. "Good."

The door shut gently in front of my face with a soft *click*.

Then a sharp *snick* as he locked it.

I stared unblinking at the door.

A coherent thought took a few minutes, always did after an encounter with all that is 'Randor' but it occurred to me…he may have used my infatuation with him to get his way—with no arguments or questions from me. I smiled ever so slowly, my teeth baring at the closed door. Julius had picked the right Elf to stand in for him while he was outside the Light realm with his Dark mate. Randor was just as cunning as our lovesick ruler.

# CHAPTER 3

I rolled my eyes and called the man who had sent me on this mission. I leaned back against the tree behind me and watched the show through the window, too far away to be noticed. Not that the two people I spied on were noticing anything else except for each other while I only had the moonlight to keep me company.

Randor answered on the fourth ring, his voice whisper soft. "Hello?"

"It's been over two months," I grumbled into the receiver. "How much longer do I have to do this?"

The man was quiet, and then he chuckled softly. "For as long as I need you to."

I picked up a fallen leaf and crunched it in my hand, my eyes unwavering from the scene inside the window. "This is silly. Not to mention, I am invading their privacy."

He hummed. "Where are you?"

"Haven Resort." The only plus was that Juliet and Samuel had also moved to the location, the antics that Samuel and Julius pulled against each other kept me entertained. "And you know what?"

"What?"

"Our ruler could really learn to shut the curtains. Especially at night when anyone can see inside." I snorted, shaking my head. "And, believe me, he needs to shut them *every dang night*."

There was a choked noise behind me, and I instantly dropped my phone and twisted, staring behind the tree. I ground my teeth together and pointed an accusing finger. "How long have you been standing there?"

Randor pocketed his phone and lifted his hands into the air in surrender. "As soon as I saw it was you on the phone, I headed out of the realm. I thought there was something wrong." He walked on silent feet around the tree and took a seat next to me, his thigh warming my right leg. The glow of the moon showed his cheeks were flushed from exertion, his white hair askew about his head from moving so fast. "I swear, I just got here."

I grunted and lifted my phone, turning it off. My finger waggled at the window I was watching. "Seriously. How much sex can one couple have?"

Blue eyes turned to the window in question, already having noticed it, his tone an intimate purr. "A lot, Susan. Trust me."

I sighed, ignoring his tone. "Are you going to tell me why I'm spying on them yet?"

"Nope." He leaned back on his arms, his taut bicep pressed against my arm. His head cocked, watching our ruler and his mate, their feelings toward one another obvious. His lips curved in appreciation. "They love one another."

"They *love* one another any chance they get." I picked up another leaf and tossed it aside. My next words were quiet and sincere, not looking away from my mission. "But they really do love each other."

The only lights lit in their cavernous room where on the bedside tables next to the bed's metal frame. And said bed was occupied. Very occupied.

By Kenna.

And Julius.

An extremely naked Kenna and Julius.

Positioned as I was, they were in profile, but I could still see the sweat glistening on their bodies. My ruler was on his knees, his bare ass flexing up from the mattress, into Kenna, her legs wrapped around his waist, riding him.

They were making love.

Slow. Steady. Leisured.

One of Julius's arms was wrapped around Kenna's hips, helping her rise above him, his own hips pulling back, then softly flexing back up into her as her leg muscles relaxed, her body lowering gradually onto him, both of them moving as one. Their eyes were locked on one another's, moving with smooth, unhurried strokes. Julius's other hand rested on her thigh closest to Randor and me, and he was slowly running his fingers over her flesh while Kenna held his jawline, his face slightly tilted up towards hers. Their foreheads were touching, their movements never faltering as they continued to slow-love one another, gazes locked, their panting inhales not anywhere near as steady as their measured actions.

"This isn't something that should be witnessed by outsiders," I grumbled.

"Don't even think about leaving your post," Randor murmured. His brows lifted, still watching the love scene in front of us. "Besides, this is better than being bored."

I nodded slightly. "True enough." Living so long…well, this did give us something to do.

Silently, we watched them make love to one another, their movements pure and simple, tender and sweet. But it *was* hard to watch. Their emotions were right out there for us to see.

Long, long, *too long* minutes later, Kenna's head tipped back, her body arching, their joining not altering in speed. Her breasts lightly bounced with their movement, her hair cascading almost to the mattress.

Our ruler tilted his head forward and took one of her nipples into his mouth. It appeared she moaned, moaned long and hard, as she tilted her hips differently. Taking his free hand, Julius raised her head to stare into her eyes. She yanked on handfuls of his hair, tilting her hips more, and his muscles visibly tensed when she did it again. He grabbed her hips, pulling her pelvis against him with every downward fall she made, their movement still slow and steady.

Kenna's mouth opened, and her forehead fell against his. And her mate kissed her just as leisurely as they moved against one another. Wrapping her arms around his neck, she kissed him back, both their eyes still open, watching the other…until they slowly closed at the same time, their kiss deepening, just as it looked their strokes were, grinding against each other with every joining.

Visibly, Kenna started to tremble, and one of Julius's arms snaked around her back, crushing her breasts against his chest, his grip on her hip tightening, even though his movements never picked up in quickness, and slightly, he tilted his head back. He spoke words we couldn't here, but it was obvious. He was ordering her to let go.

Her hands grasped his shoulders, and he kissed her softly.

Julius lifted her and let her body slide against his once more.

Kenna nodded rapidly, her expression complete euphoria.

He captured her mouth again as it started to slowly drop open.

My breath seized as Julius lifted her just a little more than normal, and thrust harder than before, Kenna's quivering body going rigid. Even from here, I heard her muffled scream. And, still, he raised her again and pumped up into her just a little harder, his own body shuddering, his shout joining hers as he seemed to lose his control, slamming them together for a final thrust, his hand fisting in her hair to keep their mouths together, his other hand gripping her hip brutally. His knuckles were white as Kenna's fingernails dug into his shoulders, their bodies jerking against one other, and their tongues most definitely tangled even as they yelled one another's names into the other's mouth.

"Christ," Randor muttered quietly, sounding a little breathless.

Heck, yeah. I was so there with him.

Even though we absolutely shouldn't have been witnessing this, it was undeniably beautiful. Julius could have crushed her, she was so damn tiny, but even as they lost control together, they held one another with need and absolute tenderness. Their hands groped to hold the other tighter and closer. Kenna's arms wrapped around his neck to crisscross and grab his shoulder blades, and Julius's massive arms enveloped Kenna's bitty frame, crossing behind her back to hold her shoulder and hip, their kiss consuming.

It was…breathtaking.

Slowly, their kiss ended, their chests expanding as they sucked in air, their heads falling to one another's shoulders, faces in toward the other's neck, still grasping one another.

I blinked and rubbed at my eyes, mumbling, "Well…"

Randor chuckled quietly and slapped my knee. He jumped to his feet in a limber movement.

My brows began to pucker. "You're leaving?"

He jerked his thumb over his shoulder, toward the window. "Show's over. I need to go."

I tried not to pout. "You sure?"

I was pretty sure his cheeks were more flushed than when he had arrived, his eyes like fire on mine. When he spoke, I froze solid—any pout disappearing.

"If I stay, you won't be able to watch them." He lifted a finger, pointing behind me. "I'll have you pinned to that tree, and we'll be making our own show."

My mouth bobbed, like an idiot.

*Speak, dang it!*

He waited. Waited for me to argue. To ask him to stay.

I choked, not able to say a word.

He winked and walked into the woods. "Night, Susan."

"Night," I whispered.

# CHAPTER 4

I glanced at a pair of sunglasses inside the boutique where I was outside standing. They were cute, pink tinted and small, perfect for my petite features. I peered up at the sign on the building I was standing in front of, memorizing the name so I could come back when I wasn't on duty to purchase them. The one thing Kenna and Juliet didn't do enough was shop, so today wasn't so bad—since I definitely loved to shop.

I may have a minor addiction to new things.

No shame here, though. My wardrobe was all mine.

I looked good, and I knew it.

I paid enough for my clothes that I had better look good.

My attention altered back to my prey. She was laughing with her mom inside the store across the street, holding up a dress that was totally made for Juliet. But true to my friends nature, she shook her head and made her daughter put it away, pointing at a pair of jeans instead.

I chuckled quietly and popped a piece of peppermint gum into my mouth, the mint flavor tantalizing my taste buds. Kenna was fighting a losing battle where Juliet was concerned. My old friend could be as stubborn as a mule when she was determined.

I blew a bubble and watched it pop, startling a few humans walking by. "Sorry!" I hurried to state, my cheeks flushing. "I didn't mean to scare you."

The little girl holding her mom's hand peered out from behind her mom's leg. She was as cute as a button. Maybe six-years-old. Pretty brown eyes stared at the gum packet in my hand. "Can I have one?"

"Prissy! You don't ask strangers that!"

I laughed outright and waved the mom off. "She can have one. It's okay." And, truly, with a nickname like that, she could have the whole pack. Stupid mother. I handed the little girl a stick, but added, "Don't swallow it, okay?"

"Okay." She grinned great big, showing two missing bottom teeth. "Thank you."

"You're welcome, hon."

I smiled as mom and daughter walked away, the little girl bouncing with happiness inside her soul. I never fed off the young, even though some Light Elves did. They were normally so full of light energy they stood out like beacons, just as she did. The mother may be stupid with nicknames, but her daughter was more than happy to be by her side.

My grin was still in place when I glanced up, searching for my target.

Kenna was standing toward the windows of the shop now, eyeing a blouse while Juliet had moved farther back into the clothing store, talking with the sales person. I snickered, seeing the pair of jeans in her hand she had pointed to before. Exactly as I had predicted.

But my smile instantly faltered when I *saw* two Elf power signatures enter from a back door. The exact way Juliet was heading, the sales person showing her where the dressing rooms were. Juliet wasn't a babe, but she wasn't old enough to naturally look…and she was weak. My friend had the weakest power in the Light realm, the most fragile of us all.

And the two power signatures hiding behind a wall weren't weak.

They weren't the most powerful either, but they sure as hell could take down Juliet.

My feet were moving before I knew it, my phone at my ear.

We were in the gosh darn city, no forests nearby. Randor wouldn't be able to get here in time. I was going to have to engage. When he answered, I was already barging into the store, the glass door flying back and whacking a circular clothes rack. "Randor!"

I ignored Kenna's wide-eyed glance as she saw me race by.

"What's wrong?"

"It was the wrong target!" I shouted, hearing my

friend scream from the back room. "Call Samuel. His mate is in danger. We're downtown."

"Fuck!" he bellowed. "Stop, Susan. Do not enga —"

"She's my friend! Screw you." I hung up and shoved my phone in my pocket, racing toward the back door. I shoved the clerk aside, watching the power signatures the entire time. The weakest of the three—my friend—was being carried by another. "Crap!"

I slammed the back door open and skidded to a halt, tiny pieces of asphalt skidding across the alleyway. I growled quietly at the two masked figures shoving an unconscious Juliet into the back of a car. "Hey!" I bellowed, walking straight toward them. "Why don't you pick on someone your own age." They were older, their power ringing of many years on this earth.

One jumped into the backseat with Juliet's limp form, the other shooting their hand out. Right at me. Light power surged through the air, rocketing the litter on the ground directly toward me.

I threw up my own hands, creating a barrier of power against the violence aimed at my person. I barred down when their power hit mine. My feet skidded against the ground, almost tripping me, as I shoved against the invisible barrier even more fiercely. To any human, it would have looked like a person posing with their hands in the air and feet spread, but the kidnapper's power was eating away at mine—just a little stronger than me.

Kenna raced out behind me into the alleyway, her eyes frantic. She wasn't prepared for the assault. Her body flew into the air, tossed backward at least twenty feet before she landed heavily on her side. Her body rolled until she came to a dead stop. Her face lifted, smeared in dirt, repeatedly blinking in a daze.

All while the dang kidnapper jumped into their getaway car and sped away.

My arms fell in exhaustion. I dropped to my knees.

I stared where the car turned, squealing out of the alleyway. Gone from sight.

A black wooden door blasted off the store next to us.

I held perfectly still as the original Dark Elf stepped outside it.

Power vibrated around his being in dangerous waves, the ground beneath my knees trembling in crashing wakes. His black eyes found his daughter picking herself up on shaking legs, his gaze scanning over her before he altered his attention to me. His voice shoved against my chest like a sledgehammer, knocking me flat on my back. "*Where is my mate?*"

I grabbed my throat, trying to breathe. "She's gone." And I swallowed my gum. "They took her."

# CHAPTER 5

Haven Resort was a clusterfuck of a mess—it deserved the curse word. While there were Light Elves running around with direct orders from Julius to investigate the Light Elves who had kidnapped Juliet, there were twice as many Dark Elves here who were furious and frightened (of their ruler.) The Dark Elves were just finding out that Juliet, a Light Elf, was their ruler's mate, hence their anger that he had kept the information from them.

But they were more frightened than anything.

And deservedly so.

I had never felt power like this.

I knew my own ruler had it, but he kept it tucked away.

Samuel didn't give a crap right now.

When he took a step, the resort shook under us.

When he breathed, the air vibrated around us.

When he shouted…Elves ran in fear…and the foundation of the property shifted.

One section of the resort was already demolished.

What was even more terrifying was that Julius had indicated Samuel *was* keeping his power under control for how furious he was. Like, he had only let a spark of it out to get his people moving. I had taken a few steps away from Julius at that point, understanding just how powerful the original Elves were. I was tremendously grateful I wasn't mated to either one of them.

I sat on the sofa inside the Light Elves den, a designated location inside Haven Resort for Light Elves to converse with their ruler if need be. Randor sat directly next to me, massaging my left arm where Samuel had stepped on it in the alleyway demanding to know who the kidnappers were. Of course, I hadn't known.

My arm was a smashed up mess but was slowly forming back into a normal roundness.

I stilled when Samuel and Kenna walked into the room, the couch shaking underneath me. Julius peered over his shoulder from the window he had been staring out of, the glass cracked from the constant vibrations. My ruler shook his head. "We haven't heard anything."

Samuel slammed the door shut. A rafter overhead creaked and splintered.

But it held. Thank goodness.

The Dark Elf narrowed his eyes on my ruler. "You knew something like this might happen." He tilted his head toward me, but his eyes never left Julius. "That's why she's been spying on us for the past month." Black brows furrowed. "Tell me who it is that took Juliet."

I didn't open my mouth. Apparently, my sleuth skills needed refining.

Julius didn't say a word, only holding the Dark Elf's gaze.

"Tell me." A quiet, *quiet* order.

"It is Light Elf business." Very soft words. "We are taking care of it."

Even softer words. "It stopped being Light business when my mate was kidnapped."

Kenna's lips thinned and she took a step toward her mate. But Samuel slammed a hand down on her shoulder and jerked her back by his side. The division was clear when she didn't try to move again. Instead, she used her words. "Julius, you need to tell us." She swallowed, her throat constricting. "There's something you don't know."

Julius turned to stare at his mate fully, not stopping her from her Dark Elf duty. "What is it?"

"Other than my love, my *life*, being taken by your people?" Samuel spewed in disgust.

"Yes."

It was so quiet in the room when the Dark Elf didn't reply.

Randor's hand stilled on my arm…when Samuel's chin trembled.

No one missed it.

All five of us in the room silent, unsure what to do.

Dark Elves didn't cry. Not openly, anyway.

They rejoiced in the people who did cry, their energy feed.

Julius took a tentative step forward, his attention solely on the Dark Elf now. "Tell me."

His voice, when it came, was whisper soft and hoarse. A sure sign he was keeping himself together by a thin rope. "Juliet was right. About the Blood Tree." His breath shuddered, his entire frame vibrating where he stood. "She's pregnant."

I sucked in a harsh breath.

A Light Elf might be immortal, and be able to withstand torture, but her body could still abort the baby if too much trauma were issued. It wouldn't take a lot either, not with the ways you would torture an Elf with impenetrable skin—only so many holes in the body to use. And right now, it was as if the baby was human, easily killable.

Julius dropped his head and stared at the ground. He rubbed his palms against his face, giving the Dark Elf a moment to compose himself. He stared at the carpet beneath his feet for a full two minutes before he gazed back up. His voice was void when he stated, "We believe it was Juliet's parents who took her. They were furious when the Blood Tree declared Kenna a Dark Elf, and they didn't keep their opinions quiet, either. And when I found out you two were mated, I couldn't put her parents in the ground. So we had people watching them inside the Light realm." He flicked a finger at me. "We had Susan watching Kenna. We never thought they would attack their own daughter."

Samuel didn't blink. "Did they take Juliet back to the Light realm?"

"No." He shook his head. "They haven't come through the gate."

"So they're here. My guys should be able to find them easily." Samuel's nostrils flared. He cracked his neck. "You should have told me about them. I knew she had issues with her parents, but she never told me anything."

My lips thinned, but I opened my mouth. "It's probably her dad running the show." I held perfectly still when all eyes found mine, intense and furious. "I think he hit her when they made her leave the Light realm. Her mom wouldn't do it, but her dad…," I ground my teeth together, "he is as bad as they come for Light."

Kenna blinked, her tone shaking. "No wonder she never let me meet them." Samuel didn't stop Kenna this time when she rushed to her mate. She buried her face into his chest while he held her close. "We have to find her. We have to find my mom."

# CHAPTER 6

I watched as Julius, Kenna, and Samuel walked out the door and closed it behind them. My own chin trembled, and I shook my head. "This is all my fault." A tear slipped down my cheek. "I wasn't fast enough. I wasn't strong enough." My brown gaze moved to Randor and caught in his blue eyes. "She's my friend. I don't have many of them."

I froze for all of a heartbeat when his strong arm enveloped me in a blur, pulling me closer against him. He held the back of my head and kissed my forehead. "It's not your fault, Susan. I promise."

I cried gently against his chest and gripped his soft cotton shirt in my fisted hands. "It is. There was this little girl, and I was distracted. If I had been paying attention to my job, this might not have happened."

He hushed me gently, and crooned, "Mmm. You might be right."

My shoulders hunched in, and I sobbed. "You're not supposed to say that!"

One of his hands ran up and down my back in a soothing gesture. "You did say it first."

I pounded once on his chest. "You. Are. Such. A. Jerk."

His chest vibrated against my hands. He was laughing quietly. "And, yet, you still like me better than any other man."

I sniffed. "You're not supposed to say that either."

"Perhaps." His lips brushed my forehead again. "May I tell you a secret, Susan?"

I perked up, tilting my head back. Tears dried on my cheeks as I stared into his fascinating blue eyes. "Yes."

His grin was slow. "I still like you better than any other woman."

My lashes fluttered as I blinked in shock. "No, you don't."

"Yes, I do."

"No." I shook my head slightly. "You really don't."

"I really think I would know." Randor still wore that cocky grin, and he brushed his thumb over my cheek, smearing any remaining tears. "You just weren't ready for me."

I stared. "Huh?"

"You might still not be ready for me."

"Give me a break." A thought occurred, and I stuttered, "B-but you sleep with other women all the time."

"And you sleep with other men. That's merely a

night's pleasure." He shrugged a shoulder and then tapped my forehead. "When I take you for the first time, I want all of you. Not just the physical. Every night and every day. Forever."

My thoughts jammed against each other, all battling to be the first to spew past my lips. I choked on a stunned laugh, my brows furrowing. "Is that why you never play your flute?"

White brows lifted. "And how would you know that?"

I might have blushed. A little. "I asked around."

His lips twitched. "Yes, that's why I don't play my flute. I've found the woman I want to be with." He tipped his head down and brushed his nose against mine. "In fact…I may have destroyed it after your Blood Tree."

My jaw dropped. "What?"

He nodded his head, scanning each of my features carefully. "I knew then that I wanted you."

"But you waited so long!" I shrieked, hitting his chest again for good measure.

He snickered. "I'm *very* old, Susan. You know this. It wasn't that long."

I pouted and griped, "It was for me."

"You'll appreciate it later. I let you live a little before taking you as my own."

"You're awfully confident."

Blinding white teeth showed as he smiled. "Where you're concerned? Yes, I am."

And darn it, I couldn't contradict him. I was his. I always had been.

# CHAPTER 7

Police swarmed the Haven Resort. They were all Dark Elves.

We had a lead. A good one. One that came directly from the FBI—a few Dark Elves there, too. And a few Light Elves, but Julius would never admit to it. The Light spied on the Dark while they did their dirty work. It wasn't really a secret, but the rulers were too politically correct to ever voice the truth.

Almost twenty-four hours had passed since Juliet's kidnapping. Time was not on our side right now when it had been for an eternity.

Samuel pulled his hair back into a small ponytail, his hard gaze on Julius as we walked out the front door. "You will let me handle them." Dark eyes glared back at each other. "I'm not asking, Julius. I don't give a fuck if they are Light. They took what is mine."

My ruler's nostrils flared, but he didn't argue. He actually agreed. "If the situation were reversed, I would demand the same." He nodded his head in agreement. "You can have them."

I stared in shock. I had never heard of Julius giving over a Light Elf. I was sure it had happened before, but not in my time on this earth. I glanced at Randor, raising my brows.

He placed his left palm on my lower back in clear ownership, pulling me close against his side. The Light Elves watched the action silently. Randor was apparently done hiding his affection for me—no argument here. He shook his head slightly, reminding me to keep my mouth shut. Today was not a day to argue with my ruler—especially, in front of all the Dark Elves aiming to see their own ruler plow down the people who had taken his mate.

Randor opened the back door of a white SUV for me. I slipped inside and scooched over, making room for him when I saw he was going to sit with me. He pressed his side against mine and placed his arm around my shoulders. He ordered quietly, "You need to stay by me when we get there."

"Where is *there*?" I mumbled, seeing Kenna squeeze in beside him.

Her lips pinched when Samuel got behind the wheel, clearly not approving of him driving us. I couldn't argue with that either. Samuel was in some mood—rightfully so.

As Julius took the front passenger seat, Randor placed his mouth against my ear, whispering, "A swamp nearby. About two hours away."

My brows puckered. "Are there trees there?"

He nodded once, raising his brows.

"Then why—"

"Because they are fucking mine to take down," Samuel growled from the front seat. "Our intel shows they haven't started torturing her yet, so no Light Elves are interfering right now."

"Okay," I mumbled, snapping my mouth shut. I wouldn't ask anything else. While they might not have tortured her yet, he still wasn't pleased with the information.

Yeah. He wanted to torture them himself.

I could see the rest of their immortality having dynamite shoved down their throats. Every day, boom. Like clockwork. He would have brunch and then take a little visit to his chamber of horrors, light a fuse and stuff the firepower down their throats, and walk away to have dessert at lunch. Just another day of the Dark.

Honestly, Juliet's parents were darn morons.

Never mess with an original Elf's mate.

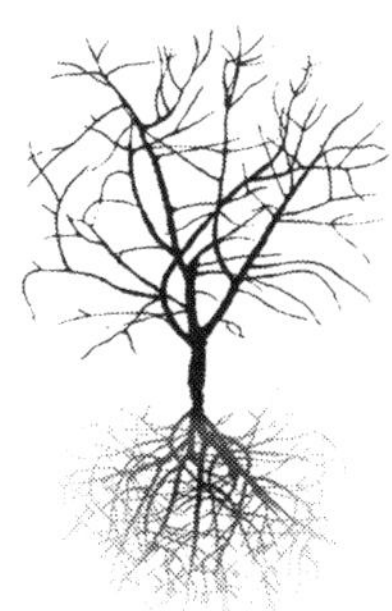

Randor shoved me behind him, hissing, "I said to stay

next to me." He shook his head. "If you haven't noticed, only the most powerful Elves are here right now. You'll need me to protect you from Samuel's power when he unleashes it."

I glowered but kept pace right next to him. "How is Juliet going to protect herself then? She's the weakest Light Elf."

Randor shook his head. "He won't do anything until he has her in his arms. She'll be fine then."

"Promise?"

His gaze flicked to mine, a cute smile lifting his lips. "She's his mate, Susan."

"Fine," I muttered. I still flicked a cross expression at Samuel.

"Watch your step," he whispered. He held out his hands to me, and even though I could easily jump over the log—I could jump over the tree if I wanted to—I let him lift me over it, enjoying how his warms hands lingered on my waist for an extra moment. I blinked when he leaned down and brushed his lips against my cheek, more affection shown in public. He grabbed my hand and held it loosely as we marched silently to the kidnappers' location.

I glanced down at my tennis shoes, wishing someone had told me earlier our destination was a swamp. My pretty new shoes were going to be ruined. I would have worn my new boots with the sturdy traction on them had I known.

Randor chuckled quietly and shook his head.

The man knew exactly what I was thinking.

We sloshed through damp underbrush. I even glimpsed an alligator.

I had always wanted to pet an alligator. It would be fun to wrestle one.

All those sharp teeth trying to penetrate my skin but getting nowhere.

Occasionally, animals on this planet needed a reminder of who was the real predator here. And it sure as heck wasn't a snapping reptile just as it wasn't a yapping human.

We were the predators.

Light or Dark—it didn't matter.

There was a food chain, and we were at the top of it.

Just as we were now at the top of a small ravine staring down at our prey.

Juliet's parents sat around a small campfire, warming their hands. Empty paper plates rested on the grass nearby, smeared with the remnants of their dinner. The small tent they had set up blended in perfectly with the surroundings, the only thing they had done right in this heist of theirs.

And Juliet lay unconscious next to them, her hands bound behind her back. Dirt covered her from head to toe, so much so, she actually blended in better than their tent. It was hard to see, but her chest lifted and lowered in a smooth cadence. She didn't appear to have any type of blood coating her mouth, so Samuel's intel had been correct. No torture yet.

I breathed a sigh of relief and gripped Randor's hand more firmly.

She was okay.

As one, everyone moved, circling our prey.

Her parents were older, so as soon as they looked up from their solemn stare into the fire, they knew we were there. And they were trapped. 'Mom' and 'Dad' had nowhere to run or hide.

They stared at each other for long moments.

Then I witnessed an event I never thought I would.

Both drew into themselves, pulling on their power.

I didn't comprehend at first what they thought to accomplish. They couldn't beat us. But I understood fully that Samuel was furious when he shot out of the underbrush, screaming, "*No*!"

It was too late. Samuel came to a dead stop next to them.

Right before my very eyes, they turned to stone. And then ash.

The grey-black flakes filled the air, rising and swirling around Samuel where he stood. The firelight flicked on his killing face, a disgusted grimace etching his lips. He growled and punched the air, and shouted at the sky, the muscles in his neck cording.

"Oh, my God," I whispered in stunned shock. My frozen form was instantly embraced by Randor. He rocked me back and forth, whispering quietly against my ear, trying to calm my frantic heartbeat. I trembled inside his hold, mumbling, "They killed themselves. I don't..."

So very quietly, he breathed, "That was better than an eternity of torture at his hands."

Her parents had done the one action that could kill an immortal.

They had drawn energy directly from the earth.

It was too powerful. Too much.

It was akin to stealing from the Blood Tree.

What the Blood Tree giveth, the Blood Tree can taketh.

# CHAPTER 8

Juliet's eyes opened, her usually sparkling green eyes dulled. Her gaze slammed all around the den inside Haven Resort. We were in the Dark section. Troubled and confused, her voice was shrill, "Samuel? What's going on? How did I—"

"Shh," he whispered softly, petting her hair back from her face. "I've got you. I'll explain everything." Whereas the dirt had been cleaned off her skin from the doctor, Samuel still wore the ash of her parents.

A quick hand went to her stomach, her eyes only for her mate. "The baby?"

Samuel smiled. A real one. "The baby's fine."

My head tilted and landed against Randor's shoulder. I hadn't heard that news yet.

He rubbed my back gently, his own chest heaving in relief.

His blue eyes peered down into mine, quiet and understanding. "I know you want to speak with her…"

I stood up on tiptoe and kissed his jaw, loving

how he stilled at the touch. "Not right now." I flicked a finger at the quietly communicating couple. "They need their time alone."

We weren't the only ones to step outside.

Julius and Kenna followed after Kenna spoke to her mom for a minute.

My ruler massaged the back of his neck, groaning quietly. "I need a bath after that mess."

"I'll join you," Kenna murmured, her eyes still haunted by what she had seen.

Randor lifted a finger, asking respectfully. "Do you have a spare bedroom here? I'm exhausted." His arm wrapped around my waist. "And I believe Susan is, too."

Julius lifted a white brow, glancing between us. "One bedroom or two?"

"One," I stated instantly. It was time to own up to what I wanted. That being the man next me. The Light Elf I had craved my entire life. "Please."

Julius glanced to Randor. He was quiet a second, and then murmured, "That's fine. I doubt the Light realm will go to hell in just one night."

"Much appreciated," Randor mumbled with sarcasm. "I have been doing an excellent job in your stead, despite this repulsive incident. A night off isn't too much to ask."

Julius chuckled quietly. "I was just giving you shit. I know you're doing well. No one is revolting—Light or Dark—at the changes that have been made." He waved a hand, motioning for us to follow him. "Let's get out of the Dark side. I have a room in the Light side near ours that'll be fine." He paused, glancing over his shoulder at me, his words dry. "I'm sure it will be better than sleeping outside against your usual tree."

I stared. "If you knew I was there, you could have shut the dang curtains occasionally."

He shrugged a shoulder. "Doing so would have stopped you from your duty." Another shrug. "And I have nothing to hide."

I snorted softly but nodded my head dutifully when he showed us our bedroom. I whispered quietly to my ruler, "You may have nothing to hide, but you do have a mate who appears to be put out by that info."

He waggled his white brows. "I'll make it up to her."

"I'm sure you will." I shut the door right in his face. "Thank God I don't have to see it again."

Randor chuckled softly behind me, running his warm palms around my stomach to hold me close. He kissed my neck, murmuring, "Are you against seeing me naked, too?"

The air seized in my lungs, but I managed to wheeze, "Hell no." I turned inside his hold and gazed up at him. He wanted me. I wanted him. "I'm ready for this."

Blue eyes dilated, darkening to almost black eyes, stared down at me, his body a hairbreadth from mine. My breath caught instantly at how utter and completely his attention held mine. It was a wake-up call to just how much *more* he was.

He lifted a hand, slowly resting it against my throat, his gaze following the reaction. My pulse sped up, not in fear—he wasn't squeezing, he had only placed it there—but in burning desire, feeling his dominant nature firsthand. It wasn't pushed on me. It was more like a slow, slippery glide drizzled over me as he stepped forward, closing the distance between us and pressing his body flush against mine. His head lowered in front of mine as he slid his hand around to the back of my neck, tilting my head back, whispering, "Susan, are you positive? I can't promise that I can be gentle."

I swallowed hard and nodded. "Yes." Yes, I was very positive.

With the words said, my permission given, my back was pressed up against the wall, and I had a hungry Randor on me, his body hard against mine. His hands grabbed the back of my neck, tilting my head again, and his mouth slammed against mine with bruising force.

There wasn't any suave seduction. This was a taking. It was urgent. Carnal.

*Needed.*

Randor's mouth crushed mine, and I opened for him immediately, his tongue hot and warm as it slid inside my mouth, meeting mine and tangling. I realized belatedly that he had showered, his hair damp against my cheeks. His slightly shaking hands tilted my head so we could nourish our need better.

I wrapped my arms around his neck as I ran my fingers through his hair. We leaned our heads back for a quick breath and I stared up into his eyes, keeping contact with him. My hands immediately traveled to the hem of his shirt, yanking it over his head. No, this wasn't going to be slow and nice. This was going to be a fast, hard fuck. I was very good with that.

He copied my actions, yanking my t-shirt over my head, his large hands immediately cupping my breasts. He groaned quietly, his eyes almost closing as he licked across my bottom lip, making me shiver, my nipples puckering through the lace. His thumbs circled them slowly, and it burned, making me arch into his hold even as I fumbled with his holster, finally getting the damn thing off and dropping it with a loud *thunk* on the ground.

"Shoes," his gravelly voice ordered, his mouth transferring to my neck. "Take your shoes off."

I lifted my foot, holding his bare, hot shoulder for support, taking my dirty tennis shoes off as fast as I could as he sucked and bit my neck, his hands slipping around my back and undoing my bra, stripping it from me before I realized what he had done. I kicked my shoes away just as his rough palms lifted my bare breasts, kneading my sensitive flesh rougher than I was expecting. I jerked in his hold and he immediately gentled his touch, murmuring, "Sorry. Sorry."

"It's all right. I don't mind it hard," I stated breathlessly. "It just surprised me."

He lifted his head back from my throat, his muscles rock-hard on his perfect body. He licked his bottom lip, asking, "Do you like them sucked hard?"

Moaning, and pressing against his touch, I muttered, "Heck yes."

"Good," he whispered, his mouth latching right

onto my rose puckered nipple and sucking as his hand squeezed.

I shouted, arching against him, grabbing his hair, and grinding against the thigh he had placed between my legs. He shuddered as my crotch rubbed against him, and I sure as heck hoped it was a good shudder because I didn't want this to stop. And it wasn't going to if I had anything to do with it.

It was difficult, but I made myself move instead of just enjoying Randor's wet tongue twirling around my nipple, to undo his belt and pants, pushing them down to his hips.

And he was hard. Gloriously, beautifully hard.

I gripped his cock, more than pleased feeling the size of him, knowing he was going to stretch me fully, and stroked up his velvety length to his crown. I circled my finger over the small bit of cum, spreading it over the head, hearing him groan deep before he started ripping my pants and panties off.

I was naked except for my socks in about four seconds flat.

Randor stood back up after divesting me of my clothing, grabbing my thigh and holding it over his hip. He took my mouth again, his kiss brutal, but it was what I wanted right now. His free hand went between my thighs. I was happy I had just been waxed. His hot breath fanned against my neck as his fingers slid through my folds. I jerked against him, opening my eyes to see him staring at me, our noses almost touching.

I returned his stare, my breath choking as he slid

two fingers into me, immediately pumping them hard. Arching against him, I muttered, "Fuck. Fuck. Fuck."

"I love it when you cuss." His thumb started stroking over my clit even as he ordered harshly, "My back pocket. Condom."

I gasped, riding his fingers that weren't relenting. Crying out, my head arching back, I didn't know how he expected me to get anything. He kept finger fucking me, his mouth latching onto mine the louder I got, his breaths just as labored as mine. Until he lowered my leg, pulling his hand back…right when I was ready to come.

"Dang it, Randor!" I hissed, blinking up at him.

His blue eyes stared down at me, his teeth clenched. He reached around for his back pocket, and he rumbled deeper than I had ever heard him before, "I want to be inside you when you come. Just hold on."

I closed my eyes, panting against the wall, and heard the crinkling of the wrapper. He cursed a few moments later, and I opened my eyes seeing that his hands were shaking, as he fumbled with it. I snatched it from him and ripped the package open, and rolled the condom on.

"If I hurt you, tell me," he ordered gruffly.

Abruptly, he took hold of my thighs, lifting me… right before he slammed his cock into my core. All the way in. I choked, my arms instantly going around his neck. I managed to gasp when he started to retreat, "Wait. Wait, just a second."

He was quivering, but he stilled. "Too much?"

My core muscles were stretched to their fucking

limit, and I understood the quick invasion had been a loss of control, but goddamn! "Just give me second."

He nodded quickly, his grip brutal on my thighs.

I wrapped my legs around his waist to take some of the pressure off his arms.

He shifted his face to my neck and kissed it gently. His first gentle action. His lips lingering on my skin, the tip of his tongue darting out, tasting me. I pulled his head back by his wet hair and stared him in the eye and kissed him once softly on the lips, nodding.

His gaze searched mine. "You sure?" He sounded pained asking.

I chuckled, and his breath caught. "Yeah, Randor. I'm ready for you to fuck me."

"*Fuck*. I didn't know how much longer I could stand still," he muttered, retreating to slam back into me, his grip moving to my ass even as my back slammed into the wall with the movement. "Too much?" He groaned, his eyes fluttering shut before snapping back open to my eyes, retreating to slam into my core again.

I couldn't breathe it felt so damn good, so I just shook my head and tilted my pelvis so my clit rubbed against him. His eyes shut then, and they stayed that way for a few strokes, his breathing deep and guttural, a soft sigh escaping with every stroke. I didn't dare close my eyes because when his opened, I wanted to see them.

I was already starting to quiver, and I knew I was going to come soon.

I ordered, "More, Randor. More."

Blue, intense eyes snapped open, and he gripped my ass tighter. He started pounding into me. Again and again, the friction a godsend as he groaned, "Shit, Susan. Fuck."

I held on, tilting my hips a little more and the head of his cock rubbed just right inside.

I screamed, grinding against him and gripping him tight with my legs.

My man pushed harder against me, taking my cry into his mouth just as the walls of my core flexed, gripping him. He shouted into my mouth, his grip changing to my hips as I launched into a sizzling, shivering euphoria.

His fingers gripped me hard, slamming into me again and again, my core trying to keep him from leaving. He drove into me so hard I knew I would be feeling it for days as his body jerked against mine rigidly, as I came down from my orgasm sated beyond belief. I managed to open my eyes, not even realizing they had closed, and his eyes were closed. He was lightly biting his bottom lip as his cock pumped into me, his shoulders jerking.

I squeezed my core muscles.

He gasped, his eyes flying open, and his hips jerked harder against mine.

I kissed him, nibbling and licking his full mouth for all I was worth, taking every groan. My fingers ran through his hair, the strands soft as silk as it dried. He groaned once more long and hard, his body leaning against mine, plastering me against the wall.

And it felt great. Really goddamn great.

I muttered breathlessly, "That was yummy."

A gravelly chuckle erupted against my neck and nodded. "Yeah. Damn yummy." He made it sound like a carnal treat, and I shivered against him. He ran his hands up my body, sliding over me like a warm brand before landing on either side of my head. He leaned his head back, kissing me. Gently. A tender brush.

I couldn't help the tiny—too feminine—moan that came out of nowhere as his tongue brushed mine with the barest touch. He smiled against my mouth, and I bit his bottom lip harder than was nice. He chuckled into my mouth, his grip tightening on my head, licking against my tongue once more before pulling back.

His smile was soft. "You're mine, Susan."

I grinned like an imp. "It's about damn time." I pinched his shoulder, making it very clear. "And you're mine. Don't ever think about being with someone else."

He brushed my lips with his. "I'll always be yours."

★☆★FAN. X★☆★

**Five authors. One newsletter.**
**All-in-one access to your favorites.**

**Authors included:**
**Scarlett Dawn, Laura Thalassa, Ashley Stoyanoff, Stacey Marie Brown, and Amber Lynn Natusch.**

If you would like to SIGN-UP for this innovative newsletter, navigate to this link:
**http://eepurl.com/bBFVlX**

# ABOUT THE AUTHOR

New York Times bestselling author and award-winner, Scarlett Dawn is the author of the Forever Evermore new adult fantasy series, the Mark new adult science fiction saga, and the Lion Security contemporary series.

She lives in the Midwest, adores her music loud, and demands her fries covered in melted cheese.

## WHERE TO FIND THE AUTHOR:

Facebook.com/AuthorScarlettDawn

Twitter.com/ScarlettDawnUSA

Goodreads.com/author/show/7141792.Scarlett_Dawn

Scarlettdawn.net

*Woodland Creek Series.*
*30 Authors. 30 Shifter Stories.*
*Woodlandcreekseries.com*

A shifter made of stone. And wings.
A human bent on free love. And drunk.
A joke could be made with those two lines.

But the town of Woodland Creek, it's no laughing matter. Hostile and magical residents guard their secrets. It's too easy to be found out.

When Isaac Stone first meets Kennedy Kirk, he's tempted to shove her off the clock tower. After all, she is gripping his private parts to lean over and see his town. One little push is all it would take...

Isaac never anticipated he'd be the one to fall.

## "MY WORLD WAS FOREVER CHANGED."

## FALL

Thrown head first into a barbaric world she knows nothing of, Braita Valorn must adapt to a dark life as a slave of the Mian society--her existence depends on it.

## SINK

Danger lurks, and Braita's lack of knowledge of the planet, Triaz, is now abundantly clear. On a mission to find her best friend, Jax, she must infiltrate the Crank Pit, a brutal complex where Mian enter, only to leave absent a heartbeat.

## STOP

Braita Valorn is stuck. She has no real freedom, her existence dependent on what the men of Triaz decide. But she desperately wants it to be, and will do anything to capture it.

## RISE

Judgments are made, an archaic stand within Mian laws, and Braita finds herself charged with treason. But never one to sit during a battle, she risks her last chance of release with blackmail.

## SOAR

Braita Valorn is a disaster walking. One mistake after another on the planet Triaz has landed her in trouble time and again. Will Braita obtain her freedom? Or will she finally accept a life she never asked for?

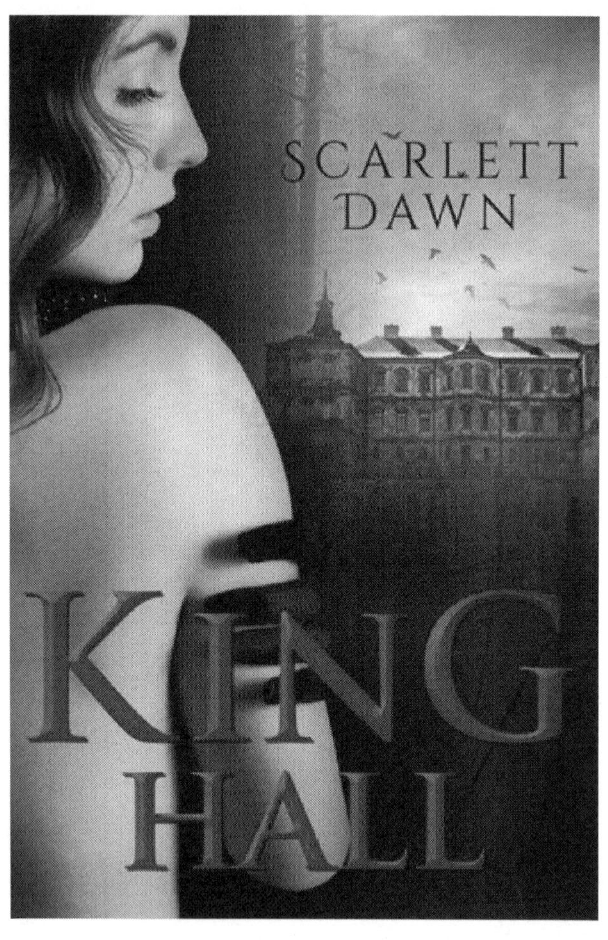


**A fresh, meaty, sink-your-teeth-in-and-hold-on-tight new adult fantasy series kicks off with King Hall…**

King Hall — where the Mysticals go to learn their craft, get their degrees, and transition into adulthood. And where four new Rulers will rise and meet their destinities. Lily Ruckler is adept at one thing: survival. Born a

Mystical hybrid, her mere existence is forbidden, but her nightmare is only about to start. Fluke, happenstance, and a deep personal loss finds Lily deeply entrenched with those who would destroy her simply for existing — The Mystical Kings. Being named future Queen of the Shifters shoves Lily into the spotlight, making her one of the most visible Mysticals in the world. But with risk comes a certain solace — her burgeoning friendships with the other three Prodigies: a wicked Vampire, a wild-child Mage, and a playboy Elemental. Backed by their faith and trust, Lily begins to relax into her new life.

Then chaos erupts as the fragile peace between Commoners and Mysticals is broken, and suddenly Lily realizes the greatest threat was never from within, and her fear takes on a new name: the revolution.

Made in the USA
Las Vegas, NV
05 November 2023

80290307R00155